SHUJAA SAFARA

THE RETURN OF THE MASHUJAA
BOOK ONE

JEREMIAH CORNET

authorHOUSE

AuthorHouse™
1663 Liberty Drive
Bloomington, IN 47403
www.authorhouse.com
Phone: 833-262-8899

Published by AuthorHouse 07/14/2023

ISBN: 979-8-8230-0569-2 (sc)
ISBN: 979-8-8230-0568-5 (e)

Library of Congress Control Number: 2023906462

Print information available on the last page.

DEDICATION

This book is dedicated to all the young ladies in the world who know that you do not have to stop being a girl to be strong.

CONTENTS

PROLOGUE

Safia Douglas is a short, thin, fit, happy, healthy, fifteen-year-old African American girl living in a pleasant enough neighborhood in the suburbs on the Southwest side of Atlanta, Georgia. Right now, her biggest concerns are passing Joshua's Law so she can get her driver's license when her birthday rolls around, spending time with her three best friends in the whole wide world, and navigating the difficulties of tenth grade. Her parents, and her grandfather who lives with them, make the core of her existence, and their friendship with the families of her friends is the origin of the special connection that binds Safia with her best friends, the ones that she thinks of as her secret circle. Within this circle of friends there are no secrets, there are no betrayals, and there are no obstacles which they cannot overcome together. Life could neither be better nor simpler for this young girl who loves her life exactly as it is.

But a centuries-old story, known only as make-believe to the circle of friends, is about to debut its newest chapter in the middle of their lives, testing their unity and resolve, spawning new opportunities and feelings, and proving to the close-knit group of friends that the reality in which they have lived is anything but real. Lines will be blurred, boundaries will be tested, secrets will be revealed, and nothing will ever be the same. As too often happens in our lives, one revelation moves us from the mundane into the extraordinary with no reprieve and no apology. Thus is the fate of Safia and her three friends.

What unexpected developments lie ahead of these teenagers?

What secrets are their families keeping from them?

Who will answer the call when the fate of the world is on the line?

What will Safia do when the most dangerous villain from a popular comic book turns out to be real and threatens Safia?

And who is Shujaa Safara, the Warrior of Fire and Light?

Surprisingly, the answers to these questions can only be found by first going back to East Africa in the middle of the 1700s.

CHAPTER ONE

THE AWAKENING

[Kilwa region of East Africa, 1752]

It was a cloudy evening, no rain. The darkness of night had already fallen, and a light breeze was mercifully removing the heat from the plains through the mountainous regions. The Arabian merchants who frequented the trade routes through this region on their way from the east coast to local villages hadn't visited in several months. Aside from a distant pack of hyenas dragging a carcass away a few nights before, the recent collection of East African nights had offered very little in the way of excitement for Bakari as he checked his portion of the border of the land belonging to his people, the Lekumba. This small, obscure tribe wanted nothing but to live in peace and herd their cattle which they used for everything from meat and clothing to goods for trading with the Arabian merchants who visited the area. The other tribes, however, were a constant source of concern for the Lekumba. The larger, more established tribes nearby were always on their minds. The Kikuyu were a deeply spiritual people and offered little threat of invasion, despite their large numbers. The Maasai, however, were an absolutely fearless people who routinely and ritualistically courted pain like a fair maiden to be desired. An attack from the Maasai would mean a bloody war, one which the Lekumba would quickly lose.

An attack from the Maasai, however, never came. Their neighbors were simply never interested in them. All would be peace... if it were not for the Adui, another small tribe who bordered the Lekumba and claimed rights to their land. The Adui believed that they were destined to be a great people by means of conquest and they intended their first conquest to be the Lekumba. For this reason, attacks came several times each year. Some attacks were just to test the Lekumba to see how abled they were for battle. Others were quick strikes with large numbers of warriors in an attempt to overwhelm the Lekumba before they could react, and it was the threat of just such an attack that had Bakari carefully peering into the dark of night with only a little moonlight shining through the clouds to aid him.

Bakari gripped the spear in his hand, an old friend with whom he was well acquainted, as he gazed into the darkness, his pupils fully dilated as he scanned the horizon for signs of unwelcome visitors. Suddenly, he thought he saw something in the distance. He glared at one point for what seemed an eternity, waiting for his eyes to discern the shadows. As if by divine assistance, the clouds shifted just enough to let the full strength of the Moon's brilliant light flood the plain, and there he saw it... the figure of an observer emerging from the obscurity of night as the honesty of the moonlight made its way across the East African plain until it fully revealed the identity of the observer, a crouched Adui scout warrior whose eyes were fully focused on Bakari like a predator stalking its prey. Bakari was amazed when the now-revealed Adui scout boldly stood to his feet, no longer hiding his presence, and began walking toward Bakari without fear. Bakari reached for his oryx horn with which he would signal an alarm that the Lekumba were in danger of attack. But, before he could get the horn to his mouth, he was met with a strike from a staff across his arm that nearly broke it and knocked the oryx horn to the sand. Bakari grabbed his arm with his other hand and spun around into a defensive stance to see another Adui warrior attacking him. He shuffled his feet to move himself backward to avoid the pointed end of the staff, slapping it aside with his good hand, and used the opportunity to run past his attacker toward the Lekumba village. The other Adui warrior sprinted forward to join the pursuit, and the race for life was on.

Bakari frantically negotiated the sand and the rocks along a path he knew all too well, wounded and outnumbered, but hopeful that his knowledge of the land would give him the advantage he needed to survive the attack and warn his people. He purposefully took the more difficult path filled with ditches cut by the runoff water during the rainy season, hoping that he could navigate the obstacle course better than the two merciless killers who were chasing him. Bakari looked behind him to see the two Adui warriors falling a little further behind, and he thought for a moment that his strategy might work. A few more jumps over rocks and ditches and he was now far ahead of his attackers. He looked back to see them in the distance, and a grateful smile curled the extreme edges of his lips as he knew he would reach the next outpost only four more hilltops away. He began to call out, "Adui! Adui!" in hopes that the outpost would hear. In between calls he looked back at his pursuers. As he looked back, he tripped over a small rock and landed hard on a patch of dried soil and gravel. He winced in pain for only a second but, knowing that he must arise immediately, began springing to his feet without much pause. Just as he managed to put his feet underneath him again to begin running, his legs were met with the sweeping motion of a staff, and Bakari was now tumbling right back to the hard ground, rolling as he fell to protect his face and head, turning himself around to see his attackers drawing back their staves to attack with the pointed ends. Bakari threw his good arm up to shield himself from the blows and closed his eyes, crying out with fear of the impending blows, lifting his voice even higher and louder into the night air. But no blows came.

Bakari opened his eyes to see what was happening, still fearing the worst, but instead of attackers closing in for the kill, he beheld the two Adui warriors running for their lives, one of them looking over his shoulder into the sky. Bakari was in shock for his life, the realization that he would live another day fueling his mixed emotions. But soon awe at the sight of two Adui warriors running in fright trumped all other emotions, and he now slowly made his way to his feet, heedless of the blood running from his arm and leg. He peered into the night as the two Adui ran even faster, screaming to each other in their tongue exclamations of terror. One of them kept looking over his shoulder and up into the night sky. Finally, Bakari realized that they were running from something they had seen there, and he slowly turned to find out what sight in the East African night sky could send two Adui warriors running like a pair of frightened hyenas who had tried to steal a meal before realizing they were in the midst of a lion's pride. He finally turned his whole self around and saw the most frightening and fascinating sight.

A bright ball of fire was descending from the heavens right toward them. Bakari stood frozen in place as he watched the ball of fire suddenly vanish from the sky. He was confused. He knew he had just seen something, something amazing and unexplainable, hurling toward him only moments before. Now, there was nothing to be seen. Nothing could be seen, but… something could be heard. Bakari marveled as he realized that there was still something on the same trajectory as the ball of fire. He knew this because he could hear it. It was loud enough that perhaps the other Lekumba could hear it. But perhaps not. The sound moved over his head and raced into the dried riverbed, causing an explosion of silt and soil to erupt from the bottom of what was a raging river during the wet season. Now, it was only dried silt and soil, and that silt and soil was forty feet in the air raining down into the hole from whence it had come. Some of the earth began to settle back toward the hole but inexplicably stopped in the air above the hole and came to rest on the silhouette of an invisible structure. Bakari stood at the top of the riverbed looking down on the incredible sight, studying the unbelievable vision which lay before him.

Suddenly, there was the sound of whooshing air and a portal opened before his eyes as a creature of impressive size entered his world through the portal. Bakari should have been overcome with fear, and he was almost frozen with fear at the sight. But curiosity soon supplanted the fear in his mind, and Bakari found himself stumbling slowly down the sandy ramp to the bottom of the riverbed. As he approached the creature, he began noticing similarities and differences between this intruder and himself. This creature had two arms and two legs, just as he did. It had a head, just as he did. It wore a mask that covered its entire head. It slowly stood up, though it appeared to be injured and could not stand fully erect. Bakari estimated it might be nine feet tall if it were to fully stand. He watched as the creature then stumbled to the rear of the invisible structure and moved his hand across the structure. Suddenly, there came the sound of whooshing air again as another portal opened. The creature crawled into the structure again, and Bakari now began to realize the unthinkable: the creature came from the heavens in this structure and had made it invisible before it landed to avoid being discovered. The portals were doors... doors on the invisible structure. Bakari watched as the creature climbed into the structure through this second door. He stood so still in the East African night that the creature did not even notice it was being watched. Bakari quietly came closer as he watched the creature open a large vessel. This creature touched a few lighted points on the outside of the vessel and the lid of the vessel began to slide open. Bakari was now only about fifteen feet away when his foot slid just a little, making the slightest of noises. The creature immediately spun around and beheld Bakari. Bakari stepped back and, seeing a limb on the ground, reached down and took it up in his hand. "Wewe ni nani? Kwanini umekuja hapa?" screamed Bakari at the invader. The creature gazed at Bakari for a moment, attempting to stand a little taller. Suddenly, as quickly as it had tried to stand, it collapsed against the outside of the structure. Bakari held the limb in front of himself like a staff and again screamed, "Wewe ni nani? Kwanini umekuja hapa?"

[Modern-Day Atlanta, Georgia, U.S.A.] 'Who are you? What are you doing here?' exclaimed the man on Safia's TV to the intruder in front of him. She was studying on her computer and liked to use the TV sounds as background noise when she studied. 'I'm a visitor from another world and I crash landed on your planet,' replied the other character in the old sci-fi flick on one of those retro TV channels.

"No, thank you," whispered Safia Douglas to herself. She picked up the remote control and held it in front of her mouth as she pressed the voice access button. "Play me a superhero movie."

"There are one hundred fifty-two superhero movies in the library," responded the TV. "Which superhero movie would you like to watch?"

"Surprise me," Safia answered. Her TV selected a superhero movie at random, and the flamboyant introductions from every movie entity involved in the movie's production began to sound by course. Suddenly, her phone rang, and the screen lit up with the face of her best girlfriend, Samantha. Safia swiped her finger across the image and answered, "Wassup, Sam?"

"Safia, you're never going to believe who wants to ask you to Homecoming!" Samantha Castillo exploded.

"Who?" Safia replied, almost uninterested.

"Steve... as in Steve Kever... as in Steve 'the cutest guy ever' Kever... as in..."

"As in Steve 'I don't study because I'm too cool to pass high school and I don't have a plan for life and I'm gonna be a total loser before I'm twenty' Kever?" Safia interrupted. "That Steve?"

"Ahh!" Samantha scoffed. "I don't believe you. What's wrong with you? This is a cute guy who wants to ask you to Homecoming. Go! You don't have to marry the guy just because you go to Homecoming with him."

"Well, that's not the way my parents see things and... well, after all these years of hearing it from them... I don't see things that way either." Samantha scoffed again, a little quieter this time. "Look, Sam, it's like this. I don't date people that there is no possible future with."

"Well, that's weird to me... and a lot of other people, too, and... you just ended a statement with a preposition."

Safia thought for a second. "Yeah, you're right. I don't date people with whom there is no possible future."

"Better," Samantha said. "You just might pass Gramble's test after all." There was a momentary lull in the conversation. Then, Sam asked, "Is that a superhero movie I hear starting in the background?"

"Yeah. You got a problem with that, too?" Safia fired back in a joking manner.

"Nope. No problem at all. I just figured you would have left superhero movies behind by now, I mean, as serious as you are about your studies and life and all."

"Yeah, well... I don't think I'll ever be able to leave superhero movies behind. They're a pretty big deal in my family."

"Yeah, I know," Samantha agreed.

"No, you don't. You just think you do. I'm telling you, Sam, superhero movies are like huge for us. Comic books? My dad has hundreds of comic books, and he even has a small, exclusive comic book club... with whom he meets every week."

"Good grammar."

"Thanks. And... my granddad?"

"Pop?"

"Yeah, my Pop... he is the biggest fan of all. The way he talks about

Shujaa Nguvu? Sometimes I think he actually believes those stories really happened."

"I doubt that. Pop seems really down to earth."

"Yeah, I know, but… you've never heard him go on. When he talks about Shujaa Nguvu, he talks about stuff that's not found anywhere in the comic books or online or anywhere. So I asked him one time about the things he said, and he told me he was an expert. Then, I told him that I looked through every source on Shujaa Nguvu and that a lot of the things he mentioned aren't found anywhere. He looked really nervous for a second and then he just said that I must have missed it somewhere but that he was glad to know that I had researched Shujaa Nguvu so much. He said that someday that might come in handy. Now, don't you think that's just a little weird?"

Sam chose her words carefully. "Uhm… I don't want to call your Pop weird because I think he's basically awesome… but… yeah… that's a little weird. But I don't think it's anything to make a big deal out of."

"Well… I found it a little weird… and… you just ended a sentence with a preposition."

"I did not!" Sam declared confidently. "I… wait. What did I say?"

"You said that you don't think it's anything to make a big deal out of. You should have said, 'I don't think… it's anything… out of which… to make a big deal'… which sounds way worse but is grammatically correct… I think."

"You're right. It is grammatically correct. And you're also right. It sounds way worse. But, back to your Pop. If he wants to be a big comic fan and get all geeked out over Commander A-Power, that's a normal thing these days."

"Well, first of all, we're not allowed to call him Commander A-Power."

"Do what?" Sam whispered back with disbelief.

"Yep. Shujaa Nguvu was never in the military, so he has no military title. If he did, why did he only get Commander A-Power while all the white superheroes get Captain This or General That? And the 'A' in A-Power? It stands for Africa. He's Captain Africa-Power. Why do we have to point out that he's black? Everyone can see the color of the man's skin."

"I'm sorry. I didn't mean to offend you," Sam responded with sincerity.

"No. You didn't offend me. I'm just telling you what I've heard like a thousand times from Pop."

"Wow."

"And my dad."

"Your dad, too?" Sam returned with disbelief. "I'm so sorry. I'll never call... Shujaa Nguvu 'A-Power' ever again."

"Yeah, it's cool," Safia reassured.

"I had no idea it was that serious with your family."

"Yeah. Pretty serious."

"Wow. So... you were about to watch a super-hero movie, right?"

"No, actually... I was about to listen to a super-hero movie while I do my Joshua's Law."

"Girl! You still haven't finished Joshua's Law? Your birthday is in like five weeks. You're going to be sixteen and not able to get your driver's license."

"I know. I know. Which is why... I gotta go. I gotta get this done, okay?"

"Okay, yeah. You gotta get this done 'cause... I don't turn sixteen for three more months and I'm ready for me and you to hit I-85 to visit my cousin in Newnan."

"Girl, my parents aren't gonna let me drive on I-85 to see your cousin in Newnan!" Safia replied with sarcastic disbelief.

"Not if you don't pass your Joshua's Law they won't. But if you do? There's a chance."

"Okay, so I gotta get busy. So let me go so I can get this done. I only have three more hours and I'm not stopping tonight until it's done."

"Awesome! I'm so proud of you for being so... so responsible."

"Yeah, well... you know me... Miss Responsible." Safia almost sounded sad at this statement.

Sensing this, Sam snapped her out of it with, "So, what super-hero movie is that playing? It sounds familiar."

Safia turned around and looked at the TV screen and let out a breathy chuckle before answering, "Well, I asked it to play a super-hero movie at random... and... wouldn't you know it, it's *A-Power versus Empress Zara*."

"Well," reassured Sam, "at least it's a classic."

"Yeah, it's a classic alright. And I've seen it literally a thousand times."

"And what's with that name?" puzzled Sam. "I mean, it's not like A-Power didn't face Zara like a thousand times, right?"

"Yeah, I know," agreed Safia. "And in the last movie with Zara, she was defeated but never found. Then, they make five more A-Power movies, and no one ever explains where Zara went. It makes no sense at all, except that maybe they were saving her for an epic final battle."

"Yeah, but it never happened, so that makes no sense."

"Yeah, I don't know what happened there."

"Maybe they ran out of money." suggested Sam.

"No. I'm pretty sure they had plenty of money considering how big the movies were when they were made. I mean, big doesn't even begin to describe how huge these movies were in the eighties. So I asked Pop why they stopped making the movies, and he gave me some weird answer that made no sense at all."

"Oh, boy. What did your Pop say?"

"He said that they stopped making more movies because the story was over and there was nothing more to tell. Again, sometimes he makes me think that he believes the stories in the movies really happened."

"Well, I think your Pop is awesome, so he's entitled to be a little weird if he wants. Besides, he's gotta be like eighty by now, right?"

"Eighty-one."

"Eighty-one. Well, at eighty-one people are entitled to be a little weird, right?"

Safia conceded the point, "Yeah, I guess. But this isn't getting my Joshua's Law done, so... why don't you go hack something and let me do my work?"

"Yeah, you gotta get that done, girl. And it just so happens that I saw a few new websites I'd like to hack. So I'm gonna do that."

Safia giggled, "You're a total criminal. You know that, right?"

"I'm an ethical hacker, Safia. And these websites are set up just to challenge ethical hackers so we can hone our skills."

"Well, you go hone your hacking skills and I'm gonna finish my Joshua's Law before my birthday rolls around and I can't get my license."

"Okay. How about this? I'll hack twenty websites and you finish your Joshua's Law and let's see who finishes first. Deal?"

"Bet!" Safia exclaimed. "Ready? Go!" Without waiting for a response,

Safia ended the call and turned to her laptop. In the background, Safia's TV sounded orchestral melodies accented by trumpets and strings as Commander A-Power stepped in front of bullets and stopped them with his bare hands, sending the bad guys running away from the lady they had intended to rob. Safia glanced over at it and whispered, "I wish I could stop bullets with my bare hands. Maybe then I wouldn't have to do Joshua's Law."

"Joshua's Law is done, my guy!" bragged David Norris to his friend through the telephone. "How 'bout that?"

"That's what you called to tell me?" Kenji Nakajima responded.

"Well, yeah. That' a big deal, bruh. I mean, you can't just skip and take the test and stuff. They have it set up where you HAVE to watch the videos and all. Just wait until you do yours. Then you'll understand."

"David, I'm Japanese from a very traditional family. I finished Joshua's Law the first week I could log in. To do otherwise would have been to disgrace my family and all that other honor stuff so, yeah, I already did it. But good for you. Now you can actually get your license on time and then you can take me to the tech fair that's coming to Albany State next month."

"Uh, no. I'm not driving anyone to Albany," David decreed.

"Oh, come on, man. Why not?" begged Kenji.

"Three reasons: one, Albany is below the gnat line; two, I hate Albany; and three, Albany is below the gnat line. Bonus reason: I don't think my parents will let me drive that far so soon after getting my license. What's so special about the tech fair in Albany anyway? Isn't there a tech fair coming to Atlanta in January?"

"Yes, but that's another two months away and I want to get a look at a new central processing unit for online gaming applications that's going to be a game changer."

"Ah. I see what you did there. Nice."

"Thanks. Anyway, I'm talking processing speeds that will only be limited by your internet bandwidth and, well, you know my family has the best internet service money can buy." Kenji suddenly puzzled, "Wait." With an audible smile in his voice, he asked, "Since when do YOU keep up with tech fairs?"

"What? I'm... kind of... tech... ish... uhm... a tech-ish kind of guy."

Kenji laughed as he responded to his friend's absurd reply, "No, my guy. You are most certainly not a 'tech-ish kind of guy.'"

"What? Of course I am. What are you talking about?"

"Stop the cap. Bruh, you know you're only interested because you want to ask someone to let you take her to the tech fair."

"What? That never even crossed my mind. I have no idea what you're talking about."

"Hey, man. It's okay. I understand. It's cool. It's cool. I get it. Sam is beautiful, intelligent, and cultured. You should totally go for it."

David was silent for a moment with disbelief. "You really think so?"

"Yeah, man. Go for it."

"You don't think she's like… out of my league?" David asked in a moment of truthful vulnerability.

"Oh, she's definitely out of your league," Kenji immediately responded.

"You mean, tech-wise she's out of my league?" David asked.

"Humph. Tech-wise she's out of MY league. But she'd be out of your league just on looks alone, my guy."

"Really?" David asked, not wanting to accept the truth, slowly giving in to the inevitable conclusion that he was hoping against all reason.

"Totally."

"So… are you going to ask her out, then?" David asked.

"What? No way, man! YOU should ask her out!" Kenji proclaimed.

"But you just said she's out of my league," David puzzled.

"And she IS out of your league. But that doesn't mean that she's not into you."

"Wait. Hold on just one second. You think Sam is into me?"

"Duh!"

David puzzled, unable to fully grasp the possibility that Samantha could be interested in him in that way. "Okay. One question. Why in the world would Sam be interested in me?"

"I have no idea, but she is. Trust me."

"Stop the cap, bruh."

"No cap, bruh."

"For real. You know you lying."

"Nah, man. She's totally into you. On God."

The realization that the possibility was real suddenly overwhelmed David, and he said, "Whoa. What am I gonna do?"

"What do you mean, 'What are you gonna do?'? You're gonna ask her out."

"I can't do that!" David declared.

"Why not?" Kenji responded. "You were thinking about it already, weren't you? I mean, that's why you KNOW when the next tech fair is in Atlanta, right?"

"Well, yeah, but that was when I was preparing to get shot down. Now, you're telling me that I might NOT get shot down and... I don't know what to do."

"Well..." Kenji thought for a moment, "I've got an idea. How about I help you figure out a great way to ask her to the tech fair in Atlanta aaaand... in return, you can take me to the tech fair in Albany and I'll even use the tech fair in Albany to teach you a little bit about tech stuff, you know, like a... a sort of... crash course in tech-ish stuff? What do you say? Deal?"

David thought for only a moment before eagerly agreeing, "You got a deal, bruh. Now, if I can just convince my parents to let us drive to Albany."

"You don't need to worry about that, my guy," Kenji reassured. "I have a plan for that, too."

"Safia!" her mom, Jerrica, called.

"What, Mom?!" Safia called back.

"I need you to take out the garbage before pickup runs!"

"I'm doing Joshua's Law, Mom! Can't Pop do it?"

"I am not going to ask your eighty-one-year-old grandfather to take out the garbage when I have a perfectly healthy fifteen-year-old girl who can do it with no problem!" Safia's mom stopped to lean into the door and continued, "And, if you had started your Joshua's Law sooner, it would be done by now." She gave a nod and a wink at Safia. "Garbage. Now."

"Yes, Ma'am," Safia surrendered with a muffled whine in her voice, the kind of whine she dared not allow to come out in any discernible way that could be misconstrued as disrespect.

She bounced down the stairs to the kitchen, opened the cabinet door underneath the sink, and pulled out a box of garbage bags. She unceremoniously pulled five new bags from the box and returned the box to its place. Next to the box was an old garbage bag box that had been recycled to hold used plastic bags from the grocery store. She reached into that box and retrieved five of those bags, stuffed them into her pants pocket, and then started through the house emptying the little garbage baskets. First, Mom and Dad had one in their bathroom. Next, Pop's bathroom. Then, the little trash can next to Pop's recliner. On to the little trash can in the laundry room. Finally, upstairs to the little trash can in her own bathroom. Stage one was complete, each can emptied, bag replaced with the ones she had stuffed in her pocket. One big bag was now filled as she started to the kitchen. There she changed out two cans, one in the corner of the kitchen, the other in the pantry. Finally, Safia made her way to the garage, where waited two more garbage cans to be changed. She changed those out and now had five large bags of garbage by her side. She opened the canister and dropped the five bags of garbage inside, closed the lid, and began rolling it to the curb.

Safia had just put the garbage canister in its place on the curb and had begun walking back to the house when she was startled by a terrible screeching sound. She turned around to see a calico cat running into the bushes as a car, which had apparently swerved to miss the cat, was now trying to correct itself. But the front tire of the car suddenly blew out as the driver oversteered, and the car began sliding in an almost straight line as it finally lost its traction with the road and slammed into the large metal pole that held the streetlamp in front of Safia's house. Safia was almost frozen as the large metal pole began falling toward her. She let out a terrible scream as she threw up her hands between herself and the rapidly falling pole.

The door to the police station in Marietta, Georgia, opened, and in walked a young, beautiful, sharp-dressed woman with silky ebony skin, raven hair, dark brown eyes, strong cheek lines, and a confident, all-business look on her face, her lips slightly tightened as if she might be a little perturbed about something, but her persona so powerful that even the most attentive observer couldn't be quite sure. She walked up to the desk where the clerk was receiving visitors and introduced herself. "Zuri Walker, Attorney, to see Mr. Jacob Tyler Mathew."

Several minutes later, the guard opened the door for Ms. Walker as she made her way through the winding maze of hallways and corridors that led to the meeting room. The guard helped her with her chair like a true southern gentleman. "Thank you, sir," she responded with a beautiful smile, ever the lady, ever the professional.

"You have fifteen minutes, ma'am," the guard replied in turn as he left the room.

Ms. Walker adjusted her chair before picking up the receiver of the telephone on the wall, and she then looked up into the face of her client. Jacob Tyler Mathew, receiver already at the side of his head, spoke first. "Are they listening?"

Zuri Walker turned her head and stared at the phone base on the wall and then closed her eyes. She took a deep breath and opened her eyes as she said, "No. They're not listening. That would be illegal."

"Look, Ms. Walker, you gotta get me out of this place. I can't rot in some redneck rat hole of a joint while there's work to be done."

"Then you should have thought of that BEFORE you got busted for selling drugs when I sent you on a simple recon assignment," Attorney Walker fired back, her lady-like demeanor now gone. "I have goals in life that don't include bailing out flunkies who don't know how to STICK TO THE ASSIGNMENT!" Zuri took a deep breath before continuing. "Did you get anything? Did you do any of your assigned job at all? Or were you too busy trying to make a measly $1500.00 on the side to do the job I pay you six figures for?"

"Oh, I got something. I got something, alright," Mathew pleaded.

"Well, then, let's hear it," Walker demanded.

"Okay, so... I don't have anything definitive yet. But I think I have a lead. Fits the profile, history and all, exact match. He works for a fire department on the south side of the ATL. I was about to check him out when I got... well... sidetracked."

"Oh, for God's sake," Zuri grumbled in disapproval.

"But I'm really sure this time!" Jacob Tyler Mathew fired back in defense. "I swear, this time it's your guy."

"You'd better hope so," Zuri came back. "Because if it isn't... I might just leave you in this... 'redneck rat hole.'"

"You can't do that. I'll die if I get stuck in here."

"Then you'd better not get distracted again when I get you out of here."

"And how long's that gonna take?" implored Mathew.

A few minutes later, Ms. Walker walked out the front door of the police station, Mr. Mathew right behind her as he held tightly to a manila envelope.

"I'll give you a ride," she said as she reached out her keys and pressed the button that started the engine on her car.

Dazed, Mr. Mathew replied, "I still don't see how you did that so fast."

"Quickly. How I did that so quickly." She paused to turn and stare at him, freezing him in his tracks. After examining him for a moment, she concluded, "I'm going to have to find someone to teach you the proper use of the English language. You're an embarrassment."

"Yeah, but…" he started. Then, he turned and looked at the police station. Then, he turned and looked at the car as the door automatically opened. He peered inside and beheld his boss, who beckoned him to get into the car with her. In total amazement, Jacob Tyler Mathew declared, "You must be one powerful woman, Ms. Walker."

Ms. Walker picked up her cell phone and began placing another call as she answered with a chuckle, "You have no idea." Then, she spoke into the phone, "Yes, Zuri Walker here. Please tell the senator he only owes me two favors now. He'll know what that means. Mmm hmm, thank you so much."

The police were moving the traffic along as the firefighters were putting an extra coat of water on the structure fire. The fire chief for the department walked up and firmly tapped the captain on the shoulder. As the captain turned to hear over the noise, the chief yelled out, "Do a standard perimeter sweep when you're done, but don't mess with anything that might be evidence! I want to catch these punks before they kill someone!"

"Sure thing, Chief!" called back the captain.

The chief walked over to the police detective, who was already writing in his note pad. "So what do you think, Detective?"

"Too soon to know anything for certain, but it sure looks like the Firefly Bandits' work, alright. Standard MO: the only occupants were on the first floor, the fire started in such a place as to alert the occupants and lead them out the side door, neighbors reported three or four men all in black running to a car in the alley on the other side with bags or sheets or… something that appeared to be filled with loot. Dirty Santas is what they call 'em. Yeah, we're… pretty sure it's the same guys, but…" The detective took a deep breath to alleviate the stress and continued, "We'll take our time and look for anything we can use to nab these guys. They use the same accelerant every time so, if we find that, it's pretty much gonna be them."

"Well, you let me know as soon as you can, will ya? We want to help out any way we can."

"Yeah, sure thing, Chief," the detective responded as he squared himself to the smoldering remains of what had been an apartment building that housed eight families. "We gotta get these guys real soon."

"Yeah," agreed the fire chief, "before they mess up and think there's no one home on an upper level… and they're wrong."

Suddenly, the chief's radio signaled on his waist. "Chief, do you copy? Come in. Chief, do you copy? Over."

The chief took the radio from his waist as he turned and walked away and answered, "Yeah, go ahead."

"Chief, do you guys got that fire under control yet?"

"Yeah, we're good. What's up?"

"Then you need to go check your phone. Your family's been trying to call you for thirty minutes."

The chief started briskly walking toward the truck where his cell phone was tucked in the pocket of the door. "Why? Is something wrong?"

"Everyone's fine but your daughter's been hurt."

The chief picked up the pace as he responded, "Copy that," and was soon running to the truck.

His hands shaking just a little, this man, who had just stood toe-to-toe with a fire at the side of his fellow firemen with no hesitation, was now dialing the phone impatiently, almost nervously, as he chanted to himself, "Come on. Come on. Pick up, Baby. Pick up."

"I'm telling you, that cat came out of nowhere. I--I didn't see the little girl. All I saw was that cat and--and I swerved to miss it. That's when the tire blew and after that? Well, we were all in the good Lord's hands then. And didn't He show up? I mean, that metal light pole bent over one way, and then it recoiled 'n' broke loose 'n' FLEW slam across the road into those bushes over there. Dang'dest thing I've ever seen. I'm telling you: Someone up there really likes that little girl. It was a miracle, sure as the world."

"And do you remember approximately how fast you were going before you swerved, sir?" asked the patient officer who had responded to the incident.

About twenty feet away the paramedic was putting the finishing touches on her job as her partner was putting their things away. "She'll be just fine," reassured the paramedic. "Some deep tissue bruising for sure, and a few scratches, but the swelling isn't too bad considering she just got hit by a… what… four-hundred-pound metal pole?" The lady gently placed one hand on Safia's head in comfort as she smiled and said, "We're just glad that pole recoiled and snapped the other way. Right?"

"Right," agreed Safia, looking down at the bandaged hands that had saved her life.

Turning to Safia's mom, the paramedic continued, "Just be sure to follow up with your regular doctor Monday morning. They may want to see her and order some x-rays just to make sure nothing's broken. In the meantime, if she starts hurting more and you think something may be wrong, don't wait. You can take her right to the emergency room and they can order the x-rays tonight. You might have to wait a while, but they can do it."

"Okay, thank you so much," Jerrica said as she shook the woman's hand vigorously in appreciation. "You, too, sir," she continued as she reached for the other paramedic's hand.

"My pleasure, Ma'am."

Jerrica smiled with gratitude as she watched the paramedics load themselves into the ambulance and drive away. She turned and put her arm around Safia and leaned over a little to get eye-to-eye with her as she asked, "Are you SURE you're alright, Babydoll?"

"I'm fine, Mom. Really. It doesn't hurt that bad anymore." Safia finally let a tear trickle down her face. "I was just so scared."

Jerrica wiped the tear from her daughter's face as she reassured, "I know, Babydoll. But… you're okay now. It was scary… but it's over… and you're okay now."

"Yes, Ma'am. I suppose so," Safia agreed with a tiny smile.

The police officer made his way over to them and said, "Ma'am? Just remember that the city will cover your daughter's medical costs for the ambulance and if she needs to go the emergency room tonight... and we'll get reimbursed from the driver's insurance company, okay? So you do whatever you feel like you need to do, okay?"

"Okay. Thank you so much," Jerrica responded.

Meanwhile, Pop was slowly making his way over to the place where the light pole had once stood as the wrecker started loading up the wrecked car. As the winch pulled the car out of its place and up on the wrecker truck's ramp, Pop was quick to look at what was left of the metal pole in the concrete footer in the ground. He stared with amazement, saying nothing.

"A pure miracle! That's what it was!" declared the driver of the car. "A pure miracle!"

Pop's face didn't say 'pure miracle' at all. Pop's face said that he wasn't sure at all about what had happened, but he lifted his eyes to meet the driver's eyes and put a smile on his face. "Yeah. A pure miracle. You got that right."

"As bad as it was," said the driver, "it could've been a lot worse."

"Yes, Sir. I agree. It could have been a whole lot worse."

"Well, the wrecker guy's my ride, so I gotta be headin' out. But y'all, I sure am sorry about all this."

"Oh, don't you worry about it, Sir," Pop reassured. "A lot of people would have run over that poor cat out of pure meanness. I'm just glad that you were trying to do what's right and..." looking over at Safia, Pop concluded, "she's gonna be just fine."

As the driver climbed up into the passenger seat of the wrecker, a fire chief's car quickly slipped into the driveway. "Are you alright?" Daniel called to his daughter as he exited the vehicle.

"Dad!" Safia called as she reached for him.

Jerrica reassured, "She's fine, Honey. Just a little banged up."

"Is that right, Babydoll?" Daniel asked his daughter for confirmation. "Are you fine?"

"Yeah, Dad. It was a miracle or something, but... really... I'm fine."

Pop walked over to join his family and agreed, "Yes, Sir. The good Lord was definitely looking out for our girl today." The four closed in together for a group hug of reassurance. Pop's smile faded as he looked back at the broken piece of metal pole protruding from the ground.

Safia rolled the garbage canister to the curb and put it in its proper place. She turned around to walk back to her house. She heard the screeching sound. She turned around to see a calico cat running into the bushes. She saw the car swerve to miss the cat. She heard the front tire of the car blow out. She saw the car lose its traction with the road and slam into the large metal pole that held the streetlamp in front of her house. She saw the large metal pole falling toward her. She let out a terrible scream as she threw up her hands between herself and the rapidly falling pole. She caught the pole with her bare hands and threw it so violently off herself that it snapped and went hurling through the air in the opposite direction. Safia awoke and immediately sat up in bed. She turned her bedside lamp on and quickly removed the bandages from her hands and beheld them, perfect and whole. No swelling, no bruises, no scratches… no pain.

CHAPTER TWO

***

THE SECRET CIRCLE

[Kilwa region of East Africa, 1752]

"Wewe ni nani? Kwanini umekuja hapa?" Bakari demanded as he held the limb in front of himself, half in threat of attack and half in frightened, desperate defense.

The creature carefully and slowly reached into the vessel and retrieved a small box with lights flickering around the edges of it and affixed the box to the armor on its chest. A few presses of the lights and the box lit up for a moment with a brilliant array of colors.

Bakari yelled, "Hiyo ni nini? Unafanya nini? Acha kufanya hivyo!" The creature spoke in a deep voice that sounded like a gurgling growl, desperately trying to communicate with Bakari. The words and sounds were so foreign to Bakari that he squinted his eyes and drew back his head just a bit in confusion. Bakari repeated his first questions with a little more purpose, still trying to hide his fear. "Wewe ni nani? Kwanini umekuja hapa?" The creature again tried to speak to Bakari, but its words seemed like the growlings of an apex predator, deep and regal. Bakari wasn't sure what to do, so he tried again, "Mimi ni Bakari wa Lekumba. Wewe ni nani na kwanini umekuja hapa?"

Suddenly, the lighted box on the creature's chest chimed a signal before speaking in Bakari's native tongue, 'Thank you. Your language has been identified. Your language is East African Swahili, Earth. Automatic translation has been activated.'

The box growled to the creature in its language, "I am Bakari of the Lekumba. Who are you and what are you doing here?"

The creature spoke in its language to Bakari, and the box translated, "My name is Sirclantis. This is my boat. With it I am able to sail in the black space between the stars. I piloted my ship too close to your star..."

"My star?" Bakari asked.

"The bright fire that gives light during the day," Sirclantis explained.

Bakari stared in wonder, the limb still in his hand. "We call it the Sun."

Sirclantis nodded his head. "I piloted my boat too close to your Sun and it damaged my boat. I crashed here on your world." The creature slid down the side of the spacecraft just a bit as it lost more strength. Bakari immediately resumed his defensive posture, lifting the limb a little higher between them. The creature held up his hand in a gesture of peace. "I mean you no harm. I'm just injured." The creature's breathing became a little more labored as he continued, "I think I might be dying. But if I can get inside that big box in my boat, I might live. Please... just let me get into that box."

Bakari stood there for a moment as he contemplated his next decision. Was this a trick? Could he afford to take a chance on this creature from the stars? Bakari was frantically trying to sort through all the possible scenarios in his mind, trying to find the correct answer. The winning thought finally came to him. If this creature truly is from the stars, then all earth will be judged by the mercy or lack thereof that he shows this creature. Bakari finally nodded and said, "Okay. Get in the box. But don't try anything or I'll... I'll kill you."

Sirclantis nodded in gratitude and began moving toward the box. He was weak but able to make his way into the back of the ship. Sirclantis began to climb into the box, but he only managed to get one leg into the box before collapsing onto the rim of the box, and he began sliding down the outside of it. He struggled to find the strength needed to force himself into this capsule but managed to get atop the rim of it again. But again, he became too weak and collapsed on the rim. Desperately trying to stay atop the rim, fearful that he might slide down the outside of the box again, he grunted with all his might… to no avail. Suddenly, ebony arms embraced him and held him up. Sirclantis managed to turn his head slightly and beheld Bakari as the Lekumba warrior strained with all his might to help the large visitor from the stars successfully make his way into the box. Sirclantis collapsed inside the box, his breathing now even more labored. He slowly moved his shaky, weakened arm until his hand was over the controls. He pressed a single button, and the lid began to close. As it did, he began to remove his helmet, and just before the lid closed completely, Bakari and Sirclantis locked eyes as Bakari looked upon this visitor's true face for the first time.

[Modern-Day Atlanta, Georgia, U.S.A.] The congregation was in the middle of the last chorus of a powerful song when Safia used her better hand to send out a text to her best friends in the whole world to meet after morning service. Safia's mother noticed and gave her a look that would make any child wither into the nearest crack with shame. Safia mouthed, "Sorry," to her mother without making a sound as she quickly put the phone away. The congregation repeated the last line of the worship song together as the organ began to vamp. Amens and hallelujahs echoed amid the clapping of hands as the pastor encouraged everyone to continue to worship. But Safia's mind was far from the worship service as her thoughts ran wild with questions and concerns of the new developments in her life.

In an abandoned building on the outskirts of Atlanta, Georgia, Safia awaited her three best friends. Samantha, Kenji, and David entered the first floor, stashing their bicycles next to Safia's in the first room on the left before heading upstairs. The small group assembled in a second-floor room that they had claimed as their own many years earlier. "So, what's the emergency?" David asked Safia, the other two friends likewise anxious to know the reason for the meeting. Safia was holding a four-foot-long piece of one-inch rebar. She extended it to David, and he took it. "Yeah, so… you've been in the dump pile out back."

"Try to bend it," Safia said.

"Why? You know I can't."

"You're the strongest one of us. Just try. For me, just try. Okay?"

David was confused as he complied, "Okay. Sure." David tried to bend the rebar, but nothing happened. "There. Told ya. I can't bend it."

Safia turned to Kenji and asked the same of him. "Kenji, you try it."

Kenji was also confused and said, "David is bigger than me and he couldn't bend it."

David answered Kenji's comment with, "I may be bigger, but you're definitely stronger."

"You really think so?" Kenji asked with a smile.

"Yeah, bruh. All that kung fu training."

"It's karate, dumb butt, and it doesn't give me superhuman strength, which is what it would take for a person to bend that bar."

"Just try it," Safia insisted.

"Okay," Kenji agreed, "but I'm not one of the strong guys that bends stuff for a living, so don't expect much." Kenji measured the rebar and then gave it thoughtful effort without bending it at all. "Well, I've seen people bend these things before, but they start with their heads or their teeth, and then they finish by pulling it into their bodies."

"Their teeth?" Sam asked with amazement.

"Yeah, their teeth. Anyway, they train for like years to be able to do that stuff. And that's with thinner stuff than this." Kenji laid the rebar down and asked Safia, "So, what was that about?"

Safia looked at her closest friends, knowing that what happened next would change everything forever. She took a deep breath, and then removed the bandages from her hands. "Safia, what are you doing?" Sam asked with concern. Safia continued until she revealed her hands, perfect and whole.

Then, she picked up the rebar and held it on each end with her two hands. With the rebar out in front of her, Safia began straining. Kenji tried to interject, "That's not even how you..." But before he could finish, the metal bar began to bend. As it did, Safia didn't have to strain as hard, and the rebar began bending faster until, in only seconds, Safia had bent the bar so that the middle made a circle. Her friends were speechlessly amazed.

Safia walked between them and threw the curled rebar onto a pile of eight others that had been bent into a circle just like the last one. She turned to face her friends and said, "That's the emergency."

Her friends marveled. "Whoa!" David whispered in amazement. "That's incredible!"

"No, that's impossible," marveled Kenji. "How did you do that?"

"I don't know," Safia explained. "Until yesterday I had never experienced anything out of the ordinary. But when that car hit that streetlamp and the pole fell over, I just threw my hands up, pure instinct, ya' know? And when it hit my hands, it hurt so bad. I really didn't remember throwing the pole off of me and across the street."

"What?" Sam interjected in total surprise.

"Yeah. I didn't realize it at the time, but I actually caught the pole and threw it all the way across the street into the neighbor's yard. I was so focused on how badly my hands hurt and… I was so thankful to be alive, that I didn't realize that I had done it. I kinda blacked out a little, I think. But, when I went to sleep, the first thing I dreamed was the accident and me catching that pole and throwing it across the street. I woke up and unbandaged my hands. They were completely healed."

"Whoa," David whispered again.

"Yeah," Safia agreed. "And then, I realized that my hands had been swollen and bruised with several scrapes on them. But it was all gone. There was absolutely nothing wrong with my hands. They were perfectly healed… only six hours after the accident."

"Guys. You know what this means, right?" David asked.

"What?" Sam asked back.

"It means that Safia is developing superpowers!"

"That's bull, bruh," Kenji responded.

"No! I'm serious! Think about it: super strength and super healing. One alone you maybe can explain away. But not both. Together, they make a superhero."

"Wait, now. That's not fair," interjected Sam. "Just because these things are happening doesn't mean that Safia is developing superpowers. And even if she is, she doesn't necessarily have to become a superhero, right? I mean, she can just be a normal girl if she wants."

"What is wrong with you, Sam?" David fired back. "Of course she wants to be a superhero. If you've got these kinds of powers and you come from her kind of family, you're gonna want to be a superhero. Why else would she have these powers?"

"Alright, hold on just a minute!" Kenji interrupted. "First of all, we don't know that Safia is developing superpowers. We don't even know exactly what is happening or why it's happening. For all we know, this is some sort of anomaly, and in a few days, whatever this is could be gone. And second, even if Safia is developing superpowers, you can't put pressure on her to use those powers the way you think she should."

"Kenji's right," agreed Sam. "We need to find out what is happening to Safia first. Then, if she is developing superpowers... it should be up to her to decide what to do with them... with no pressure from us."

"But she called us here to get our input. Right, Safia?" David asked.

Safia thought for a moment before replying, "I called you here because you're my closest friends and... I need someone to see this... to help me figure out what to do next. But I will tell you this: whatever it is... I think it's getting stronger. I can feel it getting stronger in me. I don't know, like something deep inside of me knows what this is, even though I don't... like it's instinct, or something. But I don't understand this. It's like old and new at the same time."

"Weird," Sam said.

"Yeah. Very weird," Safia confirmed.

The group was silent for a moment until Kenji broke the silence with, "Well... if you are indeed developing superhuman abilities, we need to find a way to confirm it, and then we are going to need a plan to help you learn to control your powers."

"Yeah, we'll totally go to the library," scoffed Sam. "I'm sure there's a book there called 'So, You Think You Might Be Developing Superpowers.'"

"Yeah, I don't know how we're going to go about this, bruh," David agreed. "Sam's right. I don't think there's a book on this stuff."

"Actually... there is," Kenji responded.

"What do you mean?" Safia asked in confusion.

"I mean, there is a book... and Safia... it's already at your house."

"What are you talking about?" Safia puzzled.

"Are you for real?" David added.

Kenji turned to David just long enough to answer, "Yeah, bruh. I'm definitely for real. No cappin', I swear." Then he addressed the whole group, "Look. You guys know that our dads... and Safia, your grandad and mine, too... are in that comic book group. Well, what you guys don't know is that Safia's Pop, her dad, my Gramps, my dad, and David, your dad… well, they make up the inner circle of that group. And they've got a set of books that they don't let anyone else in the group see."

"You're cappin'," David responded.

"You're freaking me out," Sam added, hers the only family not associated with the group.

"Well, it's true. I know because I've seen the books. My dad showed one of them to me and made me study some of the things in that one book, but he wouldn't let me see the other books. They were in a set in a lockbox. The lockbox gets passed among the members of the inner circle. Well, one day, when my dad wasn't paying attention, I sneaked a peak at one of the other books, and it was a book about identifying superpowers and how to train with them."

"No way!" Sam whispered in shock.

Safia was silent, disturbed by this new revelation.

"That is so cool!" David added, his face lighting up with uncontainable excitement.

"Yeah. That's what I thought. Anyway, I didn't get a real good look at it, but something tells me that it's real. And the keeper of this set of books…" Kenji turned to Safia as he completed the revelation, "is your Pop."

Safia was visibly disturbed by the news, unable to formulate a response. David exclaimed, "That's awesome! Safia, you can just talk to your Pop, and he can help you figure this all out!"

"No!" exclaimed Safia.

"What? Why not?" David asked, confused and irritated by her response.

"Because we don't know what they're going to say. What if they're just really big comic book fans and I go in there and tell them… and they freak out? Or worse, I tell them and they… force me to become some kind of superhero or something?"

"Or worse," Kenji added. "What if they mess up and let someone in the government know, and then they try to come and take Safia away to do experiments on her or some other awful stuff like that?"

The group fell silent as the weight of the implications of Kenji's point sank in. David then somberly added, "They might freak out and… unintentionally put Safia at risk."

"That's why I believe Safia needs to sneak into Pop's room and borrow that book," Kenji continued.

"Yeah, but it's locked, right?" David pointed out.

"It is locked, but… I think my dad has a key. I can get the key, no problem. The real question is: can Safia get into her Pop's room and get the book?"

Everyone looked at Safia, trying not to add pressure, failing miserably. Sam took Safia by the hand and said, "Forget us, Safia. This is about you. It's your call. You do what you think is right."

Safia considered her options well. Finally, she came to the inevitable conclusion that she must know and said, "Kenji, get the key. I'll get the book."

Kenji's father, Minato Nakajima, was intensely sparring with swords with his father, Kaito, in the back yard of their family home. The razor-sharp swords sang melodies as they clashed, sometimes even producing sparks. Minato stepped back for a moment and said, "Father, that was a little close, wasn't it?"

In perfect English, but still with a strong Japanese accent, Kaito Nakajima responded to his son, "I am an old man. It is your duty to ensure that I do not harm you." He then smiled at his son before attacking, resuming the training session between the two.

Kenji looked on at the action, confirming that now was indeed the best time to sneak into his father's study and find the key. He carefully made his way into the study, utilizing the stealth techniques he had learned from his father and grandfather, stepping carefully, as trained, making no sounds at all. Once inside the study, he began searching for the key in the last place he had seen it. It wasn't there. He looked around in thoughtful contemplation before deciding that it must be in a special trunk in the corner where Kenji had seen his father keep other extremely important things. He opened the trunk and found the key. He picked up the key and smiled to himself as he looked around to make sure he had not been detected. He looked back at the trunk to close it, but before he managed to close the lid completely, something in the trunk caught his eye. He fully opened the lid again and moved the top book from the pile so that he could see the ages-old paper completely. There, in Japanese, was written a list of super-powered individuals, all from comic books. Heroes and villains alike were listed, each one's powers and weaknesses listed in the next column beside their names. In the third column... the most shocking thing. One of four words appeared next to each entry: dead, tracked, unknown, or myth. Kenji was stunned at the words. He wondered what the words meant. Was his father tracking superhumans as a hobby... or was he somehow responsible for those who were marked dead? He did notice that most of the names were labeled 'myth' and thought that perhaps that meant that he was merely cataloguing them... perhaps like a historian. Kenji really hoped that it was only the historian thing. He was also amazed at just how many names were NOT marked 'myth.' He suddenly heard a noise and was startled, so he quickly put things back as he had found them, except for the key which he slid into his pocket. Kenji quietly left the room and started down the hallway, stopping at the window to confirm that his father and grandfather were still, indeed, sparring on the back lawn. He paused just a moment to admire their perfect form, and then Kenji made his way through the rest of the house. "Hey, Mom," he shouted, "I'm headed back out to hang with my peeps. Is that okay?"

"Yūshoku de ienikaeru!" *(Be home before dinner!)* his mom called out.

"Arigatou gozaimasu, Okasan!" *(Thank you, Mother!)* Kenji called back as he hurried out the front door.

His mother listened to the door close behind him as he left and muttered to herself, "Kare wa kare ga nozomu mono o te ni ireru toki wa itsu demo tsuneni fōmarudesu." *(When he gets what he desires, always he is formal.)*

Jacob Tyler Mathew peered through the binoculars in his hand, hoping for some sign of life in his stakeout. His cell phone rang, so he looked at the caller ID and sighed a sigh that said that he didn't want to answer but that he knew he had to. "Yes, Ma'am?" he answered.

"So what does my money have you doing today?"

"I'm staking out the fire department where this guy of yours works. He's supposed to come in at three, so I'm here early so I can get a beat on his habits, you know... trying to do my job the right way and all that."

"Well, it's about time. Are you sure you're somewhere where you won't be spotted?"

"Yes, Ma'am," he whined. "This isn't my first stakeout, you know?"

"Don't get smart with me, Mathew. You'd be way out of your league in such a contest. Just do your job and report back as soon as you have something for me."

"Yes, Ma'am," Mathew ended the call, and went back to peering through the binoculars. As he did, he panned to the left and saw a well-shaped woman walking down the sidewalk next to the fire station. "Hello, darling," he muttered to himself. He followed her every step as she strolled by. Suddenly, he noticed something in the background behind her. He panned back a little and saw three figures in the shadows of the alley next to the fire station. "What do we have here?" he whispered to himself. He watched as they lit a makeshift firebomb and threw it into the back window of the fire station. "No way!" he exclaimed to himself as he quickly sat up to get a better look at the events unfolding before his eyes. The three figures ran away as the fire in the station began to grow. "Haha! You have got to be kidding me." He waited for the firemen to notice. Finally, they did notice, and they all began scrambling to put out the fire. He realized that perhaps he didn't need to hang around too long, and he quickly cranked his car and made the block to avoid any suspicion. As he made the first turn, he glanced over at the firefighters fighting a fire in their own firehouse. Mathew laughed out loud and just shook his head in gleeful disbelief as he accelerated down the street to begin his quick run around the block.

Kenji hurried into the secret room as his friends perked up with anticipation of the outcome of his mission. He smiled and held up the key as his friends voiced their approval. His smile faded a little, and Safia asked, "What's wrong?"

"Oh... nothing's wrong," Kenji responded. "Why do you think something's wrong?"

Safia replied, "I don't know. There was just a look on your face... for a moment... I thought something might be wrong."

"Nope. Nothing wrong. I have the key." Kenji sighed to relieve the stress. "And now, it's up to you to get that book from your Pop's room. Do you think you can do it?"

Everyone looked at Safia as she tried to mask the doubt that wanted to show on her face. "Uh, yeah. Duh!" she feigned. "Piece of cake. It's in the bag."

"Are you sure about that?" Kenji probed.

"Yeah. I got this," she assured. Safia slipped the key into her pants pocket and took a deep breath. "Okay. Here goes nothin', right?" She gave her friends a thumbs up.

"You got this, Saf," reassured Sam as she gave Safia a hug. Safia's friends watched as she made her way out of the room, down the stairs, and out the front door. As she walked away, Sam questioned, "What happens if she gets caught?"

"It could start something that spirals out of control, or… maybe nothing happens," David responded. "But she won't get caught. And even if she does, it's gonna be okay, right Kenji?"

Kenji had a troubled look on his face as he responded, "Uh, yeah. Everything's gonna be okay."

The phone rang in Jacob Tyler Mathew's hand. "Yes, Ma'am?" he answered.

"How's it going today, Mathew?" Zuri Walker's voice asked.

"Pretty good. That fire I told you about? Well, I was able to park the car around the corner and get out and watch with a nice little crowd that has gathered. So, I'm able to get a close-up look unnoticed. I just look like one of the other nosey neighbors. You know what I mean?"

"And have you spotted anything yet?"

"As a matter of fact, here comes the chief now. Hah! I just realized that I can video with my phone and no one will notice… because EVERYONE is videoing with their phones. Hold on a second, will ya?" Mathew changed the call over to a video call and held the phone up. "There. Do you see it?"

"Yes, I see the building and the smoke."

"No, the guy with the white hardhat on. Do you see him?"

"Yes. Yes, I do."

"Well, that's the guy. Name's Chief Daniel Douglas, Tweed Junction Villa Fire District. He's got a wife, Jerrica, daughter Safia."

"Safia, you say?" Zuri Walker interrupted.

"Yeah. Safia. What of it?"

"Oh, nothing. It's just… it's an unusual name for a black girl living in Atlanta, Georgia. Go on."

"Right. Okay, it looks like his father, Nate, lives with him. He's been fire chief here for four years. Decorated with two medals of honor for various feats of bravery in saving countless lives, blah, blah, blah. Twelve years total with the fire department."

"In other words, he's a real hero."

"Oh, yeah. Great guy. I hate him. Anyway, I'm still checking all the details to make sure they match, but… I'm pretty sure this is your guy. You want me to nab him for you or something?"

"No! Heavens, no! It's not that kind of operation." Zuri contemplated her next instructions before finishing, "Okay. Finish checking everything and get back with me when you're done. Do NOTHING. Do not be SEEN. Do not be HEARD. I have a very delicate operation going on here and I can't afford to tip my hand. Got it?"

"Got it, Boss," Jacob Tyler Mathew reassured.

"Good. Now, get to work and call me the moment you've checked the last box."

"Yes, Ma'am, Boss…" Mathew tried to get out as the call abruptly ended. He once again caught Daniel Douglas in the picture on his phone. "Okay…" he whispered to himself, "let's follow you home when you leave so I can get a better look at that left arm. 'Cause I'm one birthmark and a couple of birth certificates away from a huge bonus. And you, my friend, are the key to my riches."

"Safia! Is that you?" Jerrica called as Safia entered the door of their home.

"Yes, Ma'am!" Safia replied, her eyes widened with panic.

Jerrica leaned around the corner between the two rooms so that her face could be seen as she commanded, "Next time I see you texting in church, there won't be any hanging with your friends. You understand?"

"Yes, Ma'am. I'm sorry, Mama."

"Don't be sorry. Just don't do it."

"Yes, Ma'am." Jerrica unsuccessfully tried to hide the trouble from her face. "What's wrong, Mama?"

Jerrica took a deep breath and exhaled as she made her way into the living room. "Your dad had to leave a little early for work. Seems somebody thought it would be funny to set fire to the fire station."

"What?" Safia exclaimed. "Was anybody hurt?"

"No, Babydoll. No one was hurt," Jerrica said as she came closer and stroked Safia's face in reassurance. "But someone easily could have been."

"Who would do such a… a… stupid, crazy thing like that?"

"Well… they don't know just yet, but… they're thinking it's the Firefly Bandits."

Safia was enraged. "RRRRR! I hate those stupid Firefly Bandits! They're gonna kill someone soon if somebody doesn't do something about them."

"Calm down, Babydoll. I understand your frustration, but hatred and anger are not the answer. And they're working on the Firefly Bandits case as fast as they can. So don't you worry. They're gonna catch 'em. It's just a matter of time."

"I sure hope so," Safia responded in a calmer, saddened demeanor.

"Awwww, Babydoll. Don't you worry yourself over that. That's grown-ups' business anyway. You just… you just find something you enjoy doing and… go immerse yourself in that. Hmmm? What do you want to do?"

"Well, I was planning on going back to hang with my friends."

Jerrica chuckled, "But you just left them, didn't you?"

"Yes, Ma'am. I just came home to get something and then I'm going right back… if that's alright with you."

"Baby, that's fine. You've got good friends and I trust you and them not to get into trouble." Jerrica lifted Safia's face with her hand and smiled at her daughter until Safia smiled back. "So, what was it?"

"What was what?" Safia puzzled back.

"What was that… something that you came back to get?"

Safia froze for a second before forcing out, "Uh… uh… a book. I came back to get a book that we all want to read together."

Jerrica smiled even bigger. "A book? Y'all gonna read a book together?" Safia smiled as her mother continued, "A book club for fifteen-year-olds. Hmph." Jerrica kissed Safia on the forehead before returning to her work in the kitchen. As she returned she concluded, "Now I've heard it all."

Safia gathered her nerve again and began sneaking to Pop's room, knowing that he would be in the den, sleeping to the sounds of whatever game was on TV today. Pop's room was at the end of the hall, just past the bathroom and closet separating their bedrooms. Safia looked around before easing the door to Pop's bedroom open. Once inside, she quickly, and quietly, closed the door behind her, and began looking for the lockbox. As she looked, she slid her hand into her pocket and retrieved the key, nervously measuring its every contour with her fingers. She eventually made her way to the bedroom closet where, surrounded by trophy-like preserved comic books on display, she saw the lockbox. She felt almost blasphemous as she disturbed this shrine of sorts when she inserted the key and turned it to hear and feel the click of the tumblers as the box unlocked. She opened the box, and there, in the very front of a line of old, loosely-bound books, was the book for which she had come: *Strengths: Classification and Development of Superhuman Abilities*. She took up the book and enjoyed a shallow but fulfilling sigh before reaching for the lid to close the box. But before she closed the lid, she couldn't help but see the title of the next book: *Weaknesses: How to Combat and Kill a Superhuman*. Safia gasped and held her breath as she laid the first book in her lap and reached for this second, frighteningly-titled book. She lifted the book out and opened it in her hands. As she did, something fell out of the middle of the book, startling her as she looked down to behold… the 'A' emblem that once proudly covered the chest of Commander A-Power. Safia's eyes were wide open with fear as she glanced up at the pages from whence it had fallen, pages which described in intricate detail how to utilize certain metals and darkness to weaken someone with the same powers as those that had been possessed by Commander A-Power. Suddenly, Safia had the most terrible thought: 'Could Pop have killed Shujaa Nguvu? Is Pop… Shusk?' Safia leaned forward to look into the bottom of the box and beheld other 'trophies' from fallen superhumans. Safia gasped again and jumped back. She looked over her shoulder as the paranoia built exponentially inside of her. She frantically placed the Commander A-Power emblem back in between the pages of the book and put the book back in its proper place. As soon as she had locked the box and returned it to its hallowed place in the… shrine… she stuffed the book under her shirt and hurried out of the room. She darted down the hallway and out the door, terrified and anxious to confide in her friends her dreadful discovery, hoping that they could provide a rational explanation to set her mind at ease, knowing that no other explanation could fit what she had found.

As she ran across the front lawn, Nate gently opened the door of the bathroom, the bathroom next to his own bedroom. He looked out to be sure that Safia was indeed gone. A troubled look on his face, Nate went into his room and looked around, searching for signs of Safia's presence. He walked toward the closet, holding his breath. But, after he opened the door, he noticed that the box had been disturbed. Kneeling down, he took the key from around his neck and used it to open the box. His face contorted with pain and emotional discomfort as he saw the missing book... and the other book with the Commander A-Power emblem sticking slightly out of the top of the pages. With ever-building pain showing in his face, he opened the book and watched the emblem fall out. He picked the emblem up in his hand and squeezed it tightly, almost angrily, as a single tear trickled down one side of his face. Then, wiping the tear with his other hand, he took a deep breath before putting everything back as it should have been.

Safia was ready to cry when she ran up the stairs to the secret room where her most-trusted friends awaited her. They stood to their feet with anticipation when she entered the room, and Safia could hold her tears back no more. "Saf, what's wrong?" Sam asked as she hurried to embrace her friend. "Hey, hey, shh," she whispered. "It's okay." Kenji and David looked at each other, not knowing what to do. Safia cried for a few moments more on Sam's shoulder before she was able to get herself settled down. Sam wiped Safia's tears with her hands and said, "Shhhh. Why don't you calm down and tell us what happened?"

Safia finally got herself under control and began, "I got the book, but... I saw something."

"Okay. What did you see?" encouraged Kenji.

"Another book... a book about how to kill people with superhuman powers... how to kill people like me."

"Whoa!" whispered David. Samantha took a step back in shock, making sure to keep her hand on Safia's shoulder for emotional support.

"That's not all," Safia continued. "When I opened that book,

Commander A-Power's chest emblem thingy fell out of the book. It marked the pages that tell how to kill Commander A-Power."

"No way!" whispered David in sad amazement.

"You gotta be kidding me," Sam added.

"No... no, it's... it's true... and... there were more... trophies, I guess?... taken from the bodies of other superhumans. You guys.... I think Pop might be Shusk."

"No way! Nah hah!" declared David.

"Who is Shusk?" asked Sam.

"I'm serious, guys. I really think Pop is Shusk."

"That's impossible, Safia!" exclaimed David. "There has to be another explanation."

"Who is Shusk?" Sam asked again.

"No, it's... it's totally possible," added Kenji.

"What do you mean by that?" objected David.

"GUYS!!!" screamed Sam. Everyone was suddenly silent in response as she quietly asked again, "Who is Shusk?"

David explained, "Okay, Shusk is a legendary figure. He's not real, just like superheroes are not real."

"I think after what has happened to me in the last twenty-four hours, we shouldn't jump to conclusions about who or what is or isn't real," Safia interjected.

"Okay... that's a valid point," David conceded. He continued his explanation to Sam, "So... Shusk was a character in the A-Power comics who went around... killing superhumans, good and bad alike, didn't make a difference. So, he was dubbed the SuperHUman Serial Killer... and they just took the first letters and named him Shusk. Until now, he has only been a fictional character, but now... I suppose anything is possible. But if Shusk IS real, it can't be Safia's Pop. I mean... it's Pop, right?"

"Yeah," Sam agreed.

"I don't know, guys," Kenji surprised everyone.

Safia looked at Kenji and read his face. "What are you not telling us?"

Kenji nervously paused for a moment before finally saying, "Look. When I was in my dad's room... I saw something, too. It was a list of superhumans, all heroes or villains from the Commander A-Power comic books. Next to each name it told whether the person was a myth...

I'm guessing that means that they weren't real… or being tracked, or unknown, or…"

After a long pause, David begged, "Or what?"

Kenji finally responded, "Or dead."

The group was in shock. Comments were whispered back and forth, some to each other, some to themselves. Finally, Sam said, "Okay, so, what do we know about this… Shusk… from the comics?"

"Well," David began to answer, "we know that he stalks superhumans, regardless of whether they are heroes or villains. He studies their weaknesses and devises a plan of attack. He often attacks when they are battling someone else, so… the victim never sees him coming." As David spoke, Safia began to get a strange, terrified look on her face. "It's even been said that most of his victims may have even encountered him several times in the weeks leading up to their deaths, but no one knows what he looks like, right? So he comes out of nowhere and, in only a matter of seconds, BOOM!" Safia flinched. "It's over! Never stood a chance."

Sam noticed Safia and intervened, "Okay, David. Thank you. That's enough from you." She put her arm around Safia for comfort and support.

"What?" David asked, oblivious as always. "I'm just telling you what the comic books say. My point is: there is nothing in the comic books that describes Shusk that would lead anyone to believe that Shusk could be Pop."

Somberly, Kenji added, "Shusk was black." Everyone fell absolutely silent and now hung on every word that Kenji spoke. "From the comics we know that Shusk was a black man. Shusk was about Pop's height… and would be about Pop's age. And it would make sense if Pop were in some kind of superhuman killing cult with my dad… and even your dad, David. Our grandparents were once the leaders of this comic book club. Maybe, inside of the comic book club, there is an inner circle… a secret circle, that tracks superhumans and then eliminates them. Back in the day, Pop could have been the official assassin for the group. His reward for risking his life to carry out their missions? He gets to keep souvenirs from his kills. They never found the bodies of any of Shusk's victims. Perhaps because this secret society of superhuman serial killers did experiments on the bodies of their victims in order to become better hunters? I don't know, but… it really fits together when we compare what Safia and I have both seen today.

"Oh wow," David whispered as he finally grasped the picture of how all the evidence came together. "It DOES add up. It makes perfect sense."

"Wait," Sam interjected. "So if Pop is... Shusk... what does that mean for Safia? I mean, wouldn't he protect her from the rest of his group?"

"Honestly, I don't know," Kenji answered with candor. "A lot of these groups become so very zealous about their cause that they lose touch with everything and value their cause above anyone and anything. Family... may not be as strong a bond as some oath or promise made to the group. And if they truly, sincerely believe that their cause is right and just? Safia could be in danger."

Safia responded, "Pop... has been acting a little strange ever since yesterday. I just didn't think anything of it... until now. What if... what if he already suspects something? What am I gonna do?"

"Just back up a second, Safia," David reassured. "We still don't know for sure that Pop is Shusk. It's just a theory."

"I know, but... what if Pop IS Shusk? And what if he figures out that I have superstrength?"

"And superhealing," David added.

"Bruh! Not helping!" scolded Kenji.

"Sorry."

"No, David's right," Safia corrected. "I have to hide my superstrength... AND my hands from everyone, just to be safe. How long do you guys think I should wrap my hands?"

"I'll google it for you," answered Sam, "so you'll know exactly what to do and it won't be an issue."

"Thanks. And... I'll just make sure to hide my superstrength." Safia took a deep breath and concluded, "I just got these powers... and, right away, I have to hide them. I don't even know what I'm supposed to do with them."

"Maybe nothing," Kenji responded. "You are under no pressure to do anything with those powers. They're your gifts. Use them the way you want to."

Safia nodded her head, grateful for Kenji's supportive insight. She thought a little more before adding, "If I choose to use my powers, and if Pop is Shusk, and if he does find out about me... I don't know what that means. He might find out and be like, 'Hey! That's my girl!' Or he may go all psycho on me and try to kill me. I really don't know. I love Pop. I can't risk losing him. And even if he isn't Shusk, I don't see the truth coming out without it messing with my family. So… I think I'm just going to try to be a normal girl… and forget all this. I just want to be normal."

CHAPTER THREE

⚬

THE RELUCTANT HERO

[Kilwa region of East Africa, 1752]

B akari peered through the glass of the box as Sirclantis lay inside, rapidly healing from his injuries as waves of lights flowed over his body like the waves of the ocean. Bakari was amazed as he watched the wounds close, as if by magic, leaving behind no scars. But the eyes of this visitor from the stars were still closed tightly, indicating that there were internal issues that had not yet been fully remedied. Bakari wondered to himself if, perhaps, he had delayed Sirclantis too long for this magical box to prevent his death. So, he stood over the box, beholding this noble creature of fantastic size and strength, wishing he hadn't been so afraid, wishing that he had offered a better welcome to this visitor from the stars. Suddenly, Sirclantis forced open his eyes and stared deeply into Bakari's eyes, studying his face as though he peered into Bakari's soul. He lifted his forearm and placed the palm of his hand against the glass of the cover of the chamber in which he lay. Bakari placed his palm against the other side of the glass, marveling at how big Sirclantis's hand was. It was as if they were making an unspoken pact to start over, to begin again with understanding and patience rather than fear and assumption. Suddenly, Bakari's head spun around in response to a sound in the night. Sirclantis looked on with concern as Bakari lowered himself and began moving away from the ship, his senses on full alert. There was an extended moment of intense silence as Bakari peered into the black of night, the silhouettes occasionally illuminated to reveal only a flash of objects in full light as the box would send another wave of lights over the body of the visitor from the stars. Bakari looked around, utilizing all his senses, trying to discern the source of the noise which sounded all too much like the approach of a predator. Another wave of lights passed over Sirclantis's body, illuminating the silhouettes again to reveal stones and rocks littered across the contour of the land. Bakari looked and listened even more carefully. Another wave of lights, still nothing. Bakari tried to control his breathing to prevent it from obscuring his hearing, trying to remain calm and in control of himself. Another wave of lights, still nothing. Bakari hoped to himself that, perhaps, he was just being paranoid. Another wave of lights, still nothing. Then, the black and the silence followed. Another wave of lights came, but this time it revealed the figures of three Adui warriors, spears and shields in their hands, as they purposefully approached the site. Bakari held the stick in his hand, readying himself to defend against an attack from three of the fiercest warriors in all of East Africa, fully armed.

The lead Adui called out in his tongue, "We claim the fire-making rock for the Adui Empire! This night will it be ours!"

Bakari took a defensive step backward as he postured, "You cannot have it! It does not belong to you! Nor does it belong to me!"

"But it will be ours none the less!"

Bakari glanced over his shoulder at Sirclantis, whose hand was now pressed against the inside of the glass on the side of the box. Bakari called out, "I will not let you touch it!"

The Adui leader called out, "You will not let us touch it?!" He and his fellows laughed as he continued, "You will be dead if you stay here!"

As the Adui closed in to begin combat, Sirclantis frantically tried to sit up and end the regenerative cycle early so he could help Bakari, but he was too weak and immediately fell flat again. He grunted quietly as he reached his hand to the glass toward Bakari again. He watched in horror as the Adui engaged Bakari. Bakari was fighting a smart fight, trying to stay on the run around the ship. But he was only delaying the inevitable. Eventually, one of the Adui warriors landed a jab of the spear into Bakari's arm, and Bakari let out a terrible scream of pain as blood began to pour from the wound. Sirclantis tried to will himself to the rescue… before blacking out.

[Modern-Day Atlanta, Georgia, U.S.A.] "So, how do you feel today, Saf?" Sam asked as the four friends huddled outside the door of the main entrance to Tweed-Johnson High School on a warm Monday morning.

"Same as yesterday: very strong… and weirded out about it."

"And your hands?" Kenji added.

"Fine." Safia pulled her hands out of the bandages and showed them to her friends. "Perfectly fine. I'm just not sure how long I can hide them from my parents."

"Or your Pop," David added, eliciting a disapproving glance from the rest of the circle. "What?" he asked in defense. "I'm just saying, you know… if Pop IS Shusk… that's the one you better be careful around."

"David's right, Saf," Sam agreed reluctantly. "Except it's 'That's the one around whom you had better be careful.'"

"Holy crap!" Safia exclaimed. "Gramble's test!"

"Saf, you didn't forget?!" exclaimed Sam in disbelief.

"I went home and… pretty much hid in my room last night."

"Well, that's understandable," responded David.

"I'm sure you're gonna do just fine," Kenji reassured. "You got this."

"Yeah, Saf. You got this," added Sam.

Kenji and Sam looked over at David, who received the cue and jumped in, "Yeah, Safia. You always make A's all the time. I'm sure you're gonna nail this test."

"Yeah, well…" Safia contemplated, "I suppose it's gonna be what it's gonna be now. No sense in worrying about it, right?"

"Right!" Kenji agreed.

"Okay, then," Safia said before taking a cleansing breath. "Let's do this. Pass Gramble's test… hide my hands… don't use my superstrength… I got this."

The secret circle of friends walked into the school building, hoping to simply get to class without any incident. "I'll see you guys third period," David said as he started down the hall in the other direction. The others slowly walked to their room in silence. That's when they heard David's voice echoing in the stairwell, "Sorry. I'm so sorry."

Another voice echoed, "What is wrong with you, man? You must got a death wish or somethin'!"

"Oh, no," whispered Kenji as the three quickly made their way to the stairwell and looked down at David, who was pinned to the wall and held up off the ground by the grip of the dark, scar-riddled hands of JayJay Man, leader of a small gang of students who ruled the tenth-grade portion of the high school building.

"You got a problem, Norris?" JayJay demanded of David.

"No. No problem at all," David replied with absolute compliance.

"Good! Cuz this is none of your stinkin' business," JayJay concluded as he let David down and relinquished his hold on him. David was happy to be alive and ready to make a hasty retreat... until he noticed the little kid in the floor of the stairwell who had apparently taken a beating already. David froze as he beheld the poor kid, a scrawny tenth grader who probably didn't even weigh a hundred and fifty pounds, as JayJay Man's girlfriend, Angry Angie, leaned over and laid another punch in the poor kid's gut, eliciting a terrible exhalation of tormentous pain. JayJay glanced back at David and said, "I thought you were moving on, Norris. You got a problem?" he demanded as he got up in David's face. "Huh?" At this point, Angry Angie and the two other members of their gang positioned themselves behind JayJay.

David's friends slowly, and carefully, positioned themselves behind David, Kenji touching him on the shoulder and pulling him back just a bit. Safia looked down at the kid who had been beaten. She took a deep breath and held out her hand to him as she beckoned, "Come on. This stairwell belongs to these guys. You need to respect their turf and come with us."

Angry Angie stepped in between and declared, "Oh, no! He doesn't get away that easy! He disrespected my whole crew, and he has to pay."

"Don't you think he's paid enough?" inquired Safia.

"Yeah, I mean... look at him." Sam added, motioning toward him with her hand. "He's a pathetic wreck. I don't think he's EVER gonna mess with you guys again." Sam reached for his hand as she added, "Ain't that right, kid?"

The kid nodded his head in total agreement and reached for Sam's hand as he tried to stand to his feet.

Angry Angie slapped his hand down and stared Sam in the face as she decreed, "He ain't learned nothin' until I say he's learned."

But Sam took his hand anyway and pulled him up the stairs. As she did, Angry Angie stepped in between to block the act and pushed Sam backward. Before she knew it, Safia was standing in between, breathing nervously, almost surprised by her action. Angry Angie suddenly forgot all about the little kid and Sam as she now got face to face with Safia and stared her down. "Now, I know you don't want none of this, Douglas. Do ya? Huh? Do ya?"

Safia bravely and wisely replied, "No, I don't. I don't want none of any of you. I just want us all to get to class before we're late. I don't want to get a tardy... especially on a Monday. You know, Monday is the first day of the week and I really, REALLY need a good start to my week."

"Oh, yeah?" Angry Angie asked with a smile. Then, Angry Angie laid a hard hook punch right across Safia's mouth, sending her to the floor out in the hallway.

JayJay hooped and hollered in approval with his hands over his mouth, gyrating side to side, "Whoo hoo hoo hoo hoo! K.O.!" Then, seeing a crowd coming to inspect the action, he tapped Angry Angie and said, "Let's get out of here."

The gang quickly made their exit down the stairwell as several students came over to see what the ruckus was about. Safia laid there in the floor, her lip bleeding and beginning to swell. "Great!" she whispered as her friends helped her to her feet.

"That was incredible!" the kid said. "You guys are life savers!"

"Yeah," Safia responded in dejection. "Don't mention it."

"Come on, Saf," Sam whispered as they started toward the bathroom.

A few students pulled out their cellphones and were about to take pictures of Safia and the other student. "STOP IT!" David shouted. "If I so much as even THINK you're taking a picture or a video or... anything, I'll beat the daylights out of you... and I'll flush your phone down the toilet when I'm done. On God."

Everyone was so startled by David's stern demeanor, something which no one had ever seen from him before, that they actually did as he told them. The other victim said, "Come on. We gotta tell the office."

"NO!" Safia exclaimed.

"But… we have to tell someone…" the other student tried to say.

"No!" Sam demanded. "You can never tell ANYONE about what happened here today."

"But… I don't understand. You guys won't get in any trouble. You didn't do anything wrong. You guys didn't even throw a punch or nothin' like that." The student puzzled for a moment before concluding, "You're… my heroes."

Safia chuckled in self-loathing doubt as she mumbled, "Some hero." The crew continued down the hall, leaving the other student standing alone in confusion and disbelief. As they continued toward the bathroom, Safia touched her lip with her fingertips, feeling the split on her upper lip. She turned her head toward her friends as she walked and decided, "I don't know, guys. Superhealing and superstrength, yeah. Superhero? Not hardly. I don't know what I was thinking."

"I know what you were thinking," David answered sincerely. "You… and Sam… were thinking that someone was being mistreated… and you couldn't just stand by and do nothing. That sounds like heroes to me."

Safia smiled, and then winced in pain as the smile made her lip hurt even more. Then, she added, "Hero? Okay. But superhero? Not so much."

The telephone at the fire chief's desk rang. "Chief Douglas," Daniel Douglas answered.

"Yeah, uh… Chief Douglas? I'm a concerned citizen who's worried about these Firefly Bandits I heard so much about. I gotta know. Is it true that they set fire to the fire station?"

"Well, first of all, can I have your name, please?"

"Uh, no. I prefer to remain anonymous. I'm just concerned that I might be next. So I want to know what happened at the fire station."

Daniel Douglas took a deep breath and chose his words carefully. "Well, you have the right to remain anonymous if you like. That's okay by me. Just know this: I cannot comment on the identity of the perpetrators of these crimes singularly or collectively. I can report to you that someone did set fire to the fire station. I can also report that the damage was minimal and no one was hurt. I can also report that our hidden security cameras were running both inside and outside the building. And I can assure you that, when we take a look at the recordings and identify the responsible parties, we will prosecute them to the fullest extent of the law. Beyond that, I am not permitted to say anything else. Do you by any chance have any knowledge of the identity of those responsible for the station fire?"

"Oh, no. No, I wouldn't know anything about that. I'm just afraid for my home is all. You can understand my concern, can't you? I mean, if the fire station can fall victim to these Firefly Bandits, anyone can, right?"

Daniel drew a deep breath before responding, "I assure you, Ma'am, their days are numbered. They've gone too far this time and made a terrible mistake. We'll find them. And we'll stop them. In the meantime, if you want to, you can give me your address and we'll be glad to keep an extra watchful eye on your home if you'd like."

"Oh, no, that... that won't be necessary. But I appreciate the offer."

"Well, it stands anytime you deem it necessary. Just call here and any of us will be glad to take your information," the chief reassured.

"Okay. Thank you so much."

"Mmm hmm. Have a good one." The chief was glad to hang up the phone and end the conversation.

As he did, his first deputy chief, Anthony Hayes, walked into the room and asked, "Who was that on the phone, Chief?"

"Another concerned citizen diggin' for dirt," he replied with much cynicism. "I'm afraid we'll be getting a lot of those calls until we can catch these guys. Any word from Deputy Fire Marshall Grant on what the cameras caught?"

"Nothing yet. But that probably means that there's something there and they're trying to get a good look at it."

"Well, I wish they'd hurry it up, because I don't like being Fire Chief for this district with the responsibility of five stations... and the one station, the ONE station they hit... is the one where my desk is... just five blocks from my house. I almost feel like it was a personal attack on me."

"Hey, Chief, come on. You're making something out of nothing. These guys, these... Fireflies? They're just a bunch of two-bit nobodies making things up as they go. They have no idea what they're doing, they obviously have no regard for human life... and they probably think they're a bunch of geniuses. But we know the truth, huh? They've left a string of evidence a mile long behind at every crime scene. If we can pin just one… just ONE of those fires on them… we got 'em for 'em all… every last fire they set, we got 'em. Now, I ask you: does that sound like a group of guys who have something personal with you, or does it sound like a bunch of young punks just a few days away from county lockup?"

"I know, but… I don't want to wait around for something to go wrong before we get them. I don't want another fire. Not ONE. And, dear God, what if next time someone dies? Oh, Lord Jesus, please don't let anyone die from these… idiots," he prayed in a whisper.

Concerned, First Deputy Fire Chief Hayes reassured his mentor, "Chief? Don't you worry. We're gonna nail these punks."

Fire Chief Daniel Douglas nodded his head in agreement, "Yeah… you're right." Snapping out of the moment, he looked around at the paperwork on his desk which awaited him and concluded, "I need to get busy. This stuff isn't filling itself out. Let me know the moment you hear from the deputy fire marshal and tell Lamar to check the fuel in his truck because Joe took it around to several schools Friday."

"Will do, Chief."

Safia stood in the girls' bathroom and looked in the mirror at her lip. It was busted open pretty badly from the strike Angry Angie had landed. Safia whispered to herself, "Well, now I know why they call her Angry Angie." She tore off the corner of a piece of paper towel and began dabbing the cut on her lip. It was a deep cut, the kind that stings like fire for days. As she beheld herself, she realized that she didn't want anyone to see her like this.

Sam came up behind her and said, "Wow. That looks like it hurts a lot."

"It looks worse than it feels. What am I gonna do about it?"

"It'll heal," Sam reassured.

"Yeah, that's the problem," Safia explained. "It might heal… really, really fast. How am I going to explain a deep cut in my lip one day… and nothing wrong at all the next day?"

"Holy crap! I hadn't thought about that." Sam thought for a moment and then exploded with a loud whisper, "Oooh, I got it." She reached into her book bag an retrieved a mask. "Say no to covid, right?"

Safia had a curious, strange look on her face as she took the mask from her friend and put it on her face. Looking into the mirror, she beheld herself, bright eyes, perfect hair… a mask covering her mouth inscribed with the words, '6 Feet Apart.' "Oh, well. At least this way no one can see my lip."

"And tomorrow you'll be better, and no one will ever know, right?"

Safia thought for a second more and then turned and gave Sam a high five. Suddenly, the bell rang. "Oh, no. We're late." The two girls ran out the door of the bathroom, scurrying down the hallway.

They abruptly exploded into the classroom, eliciting a disapproving look from Mrs. Gramble. The room was silent, and the two girls stood still for a moment before walking to their desks. "Not so fast, ladies," Mrs. Gramble moaned. "You're late. Why are you late?"

"Uh… I was in the bathroom and lost track of time," Sam replied.

"Mmm hmm. Is that so? And why were you late, Ms. Douglas?"

"Uhm… I was in the bathroom, too. We both lost track of time."

"What was that? I can't hear you with that mask on. Why in the world are you wearing that mask?"

"Uhm, you know. Doing my part to stop the spread of covid, right?"

The class giggled at Safia's response. Mrs. Gramble, however, did not find it so funny. "Well, I would never discourage anyone from health safety, Ms. Douglas. It's just that… I haven't seen you wear one of those masks in over a year." The class giggled again, a little softer this time. "In fact, you'd be more at risk of catching monkey pox than covid these days." The class exploded with giggles at this comment. "I was just curious as to your reason for the sudden concern regarding airborne illness. Could you please enlighten me, Ms. Douglas?"

Safia was stunned. She drew a complete blank. Then, to her dismay, one of the students volunteered, "She's wearing the mask to cover up that busted lip she got fighting this morning." The class let out a collective 'ooh.'

"Fighting? Ms. Douglas, were you fighting this morning?"

Safia, normally a very honest person, was caught off guard and quickly answered, "No, Ma'am. I wasn't fighting."

The information volunteer, Jimmy, fired back, "Liar. We all saw it."

"Jimmy!" Mrs. Gramble interjected. "That is a harsh word, one which had better not make the journey from your lips to my ears again." Jimmy sunk his head low, still grinning a little that he had let the secret out. Mrs. Gramble turned her attention back to Safia. "Ms. Douglas, your classmate seems to believe that he witnessed a fight in which you were involved. He also claims that you are wearing that mask to cover a busted lip which you received in that selfsame fight. I find myself more and more curious by the moment. Did anyone else see Ms. Douglas fight this morning?" Mrs. Gramble surveyed the room as a few hands slowly went up. "I see. And of those who saw the fight, how many saw the other person strike Ms. Douglas in the lip and cut it open?" Those same hands went up again, a little more quickly this time. "I see. So, Ms. Douglas, allow me to explain where we find ourselves this morning. Several of your friends have signified by show of hand that they witnessed a fight this morning, and they have further signified that they witnessed an injury to your lip. There are several plausible explanations for this. They could have all imagined this, making them the victims of mass delusion and the subjects of a fascinating new scientific discovery. They could all be lying to me and placing their futures in great jeopardy. They could be telling the truth, which would indicate that a student whom I have never doubted for a moment is now, somehow, capable of lying to me in an intent to cover up a fight on school grounds in which she was a participant. I know of one simple way to resolve this issue. For the briefest of moments, if you will, simply remove your mask long enough for us to see your lips. If they're fine, well, then I need to figure out whether to call four sets of parents or a specialist in sociology who can aid me in determining how four students experienced the same delusional episode. So... how about it? Would you remove your mask for just a moment?"

Kenji spoke up, "Mrs. Gramble. Don't you think this takes away from Safia's right to protect herself from illnesses? I mean..."

Mrs. Gramble help up her finger to indicate total silence. "Ms. Douglas, it appears that Mr. Nakajima is concerned for your health. So, why don't you come to the front of the class where no one else has been all morning... and then remove your mask?"

The three friends were overcome with nerves as Safia made her way to the front of the class. Realizing that the revelation was inevitable, Safia closed her eyes, fought back tears, and pulled the mask down. She heard the class let out 'whoas' and 'no ways' as she displayed her lips to all in the room. "But I swear to you, Mrs. Gramble, on God," Jimmy exploded, "her lip was busted... and there was blood everywhere." Safia's eyes popped open, and she immediately reached her fingertips to the place where the cut had been... only to find perfect, smooth skin.

The class was now in a small uproar as Mrs. Gramble tried to regain control. "Alright, class, that's enough." They continued to chatter softly until she walked to the middle of the room with her index finger held up, calling for silence again. The room, in turn, responded with absolute silence. "Ms. Douglas, my apologies. Mr. Willis, won't you join me in the hallway, please? Thank you."

As Jimmy Willis went out into the hallway with Mrs. Gramble, the three members of the secret circle huddled at their seats. "OMG, Saf!" Sam exclaimed in a barely controlled whisper. "That fight was like ten minutes ago... and your lip is already healed? I mean, it's perfect. There's not even a scar or nothin' like that."

"Yeah, but now half the class knows something's up with me."

"No, Safia," reassured Kenji. "Not half the class, just four people."

"Yeah, but now Jimmy is in big trouble for lying to Mrs. Gramble... only he didn't lie."

"Yeah," disagreed Sam, "but Jimmy is a busybody, he's always up in people's business... I say he had it coming. He shouldn't have tried to rat you out."

"Yeah, but... it still isn't right that I lied and got away with it. I don't like this."

Sam fired back, "Yeah, but this is better than you getting found out by an adult. With other kids, it's a matter of your word against them. But, with adults, it's not so simple. So, yeah, you might feel bad that Jimmy got in trouble today. But trust me... this is better than the alternative."

Mrs. Gramble and Jimmy came back into the room. Jimmy went to the front of the class and spoke loudly and clearly as he said, "I apologize to everyone for leading my classmates in this lie. And I'm sorry, Safia, for lying on you."

"Lying about you," Mrs. Gramble corrected.

"Lying about you."

"That's good, Jimmy. Take your seat now so we can get started with our test." Several of the students let out 'aws' and 'mans' as they cleared their desks.

As Jimmy went by Safia's desk, he whispered, "You know I didn't lie."

Safia looked around at her two friends as if to say, 'What are we going to do now?'

"Hey, Pop?" came the call down the hall.

"In here!" came the answer.

Jerrica stuck her head in the door of Pop's bedroom. "I just wanted to let you know I had come home to pick up some things I needed for work. I didn't want you to hear me and think that there was an intruder or something, you know?"

"Uh, yeah. Thanks. That's so considerate of you... which is why you're my favorite daughter." Nate showed her a big, loving grin.

Jerrica chuckled and said, "Pop, I'm your only daughter. And I wouldn't even be that if Daniel hadn't married me."

"Oh, nonsense. If Daniel hadn't married you, I would have just adopted you. You know you're the best thing that ever happened to my son."

Jerrica smiled, grateful for her perfect family. Then she politely asked, "So, what have you been doing today?"

"Oh, nothing much, just... looking over some old comic book stuff."

"Can I see?" Jerrica asked, not really interested in comics, but interested in whatever Pop was interested in.

"Oh, it's nothing special," Pop answered, trying to deter her interest.

"No, really. I'm in a comic book family, right?" she pushed as she took the book from his hand and read the name on the cover. *"A History of Shujaa Powers, Powers Combinations, Strengths, and Weaknesses.* What... stimulating reading that must be," she said as she forced out a smile. Then, her face exploded with glee as she handed the book back to him and concluded, "I guess I'll never have the level of interest y'all have with this stuff. But, that title makes it sound like there was more than one Shujaa. It's Shujaa Nguvu, right?"

"Yes, but he was not the only Shujaa. There have been many called Shujaa. Shujaa Nguvu you know, but there was also Shujaa Jabali, the hero strong as a rock; Shujaa Kabili, the hero noble and courageous; and even

Shujaa Jasiri, the heroine bold and daring. And then, of course, there's the legend of Shujaa Safara, the mythical Warrior of Fire and Light, but he or she never existed… just a… fairytale or… wishful thinking. Anyway, it all goes all the way back to Shujaa Bakari, the first Shujaa. The Mashujaa are a long line of superhumans, each with their own unique combination of Shujaa powers… and weaknesses. Sometimes, I like to study up… just in case one of my buddies tries to pull a trivia question on me and there's a classic comic book at stake."

"Well, I don't know of anyone who could possibly know more about this stuff than you, Pop, so… study on, if you must. But I promise I won't be betting some $500.00 comic book against your knowledge."

"And well you shouldn't, my dear. Never bet against me… because I always win," he said as Jerrica gave him a kiss on the forehead and darted out the door on the way back to work. Pop whispered to himself, "Yep. I always win… no matter what it costs me." As he said this to himself, he looked down at the book and opened it again to the place he had marked. There, on the pages which lay before him, were an explanation of the Shujaa power of superhealing… and how it can be overcome.

"I assure you, Ma'am. We are doing everything within our power to catch these guys before they do any more damage." Fire Chief Daniel Douglas was a little sterner with his voice than before, but still within the boundaries of control and certainly laced with tones of diplomacy. "Yes, Ma'am. I appreciate that." He hung up the phone and let out a deep breath as First Deputy Fire Chief Anthony Hayes knocked on the door. "Come in," Daniel said as if giving up on the idea of fighting.

"Just heard from Deputy Fire Marshall Grant."

Daniel Douglas perked up immediately as he responded, "And?"

"And they definitely have something on security footage. They're putting it through enhancement software now so they can get a better look, but he said he hopes to have something substantial within the hour and he'll call you when he does."

"Finally!" Daniel exclaimed. "Now we're gettin' somewhere."

"And not a moment too soon, right?" Hayes added.

"You're telling me!?! And I swear, I think that's the third time that one specific lady has called. She's driving me NUTS! If we don't nail these bums soon I'm probably gonna lose my job when I go off on her."

"Oh, come on, Chief. One little lady can't be all THAT bad, right?"

At a hotel on the other side of Atlanta, Zuri Walker held her phone in her hand, staring at it. "I should be ashamed of myself for the torture through which I have put that man today, but it's all part of the plan. Mathew, I have verified several times now that the target is in fact at his desk at the fire station in Tweed Junction Villa. I want you to deliver this package to him personally. Have him sign for it with this pen. It has to be with this pen. Do not touch the pen yourself except by the chrome tip. Do you understand?"

"Yes, Ma'am, Ms. Walker. Deliver it personally, have him sign for it, make sure he uses this pen, I don't touch anything but the chrome part."

"Right, and don't forget to bring it back to me..." Mathew had a confused look on his face as she explained, "the pen..." Mathew made a gesture with his mouth and a nod of his face to indicate he understood as she reiterated, "I need the pen... have him sign for the package with the pen and then bring me the pen. Got it?"

"Yes, Ma'am. Got it."

Jacob Tyler Mathew headed toward the door of the hotel before his boss called after him, "And, Mr. Mathew? Don't mess this up. If you get sidetracked and mess this up, by the time I'm finished dealing with you, you'll wish you were rotting in that Cobb County jail cell again. Got it?"

Mathew's face was very sincere, displaying the gravity of the threat he had just received as he responded, "Yes, Ma'am. I swear I got this."

"You'd better."

As the students made their way back to class from mid-morning break, Safia asked her teacher, "Ms. Sawyer, can I go to the bathroom?"

"Ooh, me, too, Ms. Sawyer," added Sam. "Can I go, too? Please?"

Ms. Sawyer, a very reasonable teacher, smiled at them and simply said, "You got five minutes, ladies. Hurry."

"Thank you," they both said in unison as they scurried off to the girl's bathroom.

Once inside the bathroom, the girls quickly bypassed the first two stalls as Sam went into the third stall and Safia the fourth and final stall.

But the door to Safia's stall had only closed halfway before an arm slammed into the catch area, stopping the door from closing. Safia jumped at the startling event as she watched Angry Angie push the door open with her other hand. As she grabbed a fistful of Safia's shirt, she began twisting her fist around the material and pulling Safia out of the stall. "My hand is still hurting from where I hit your ugly mug. And what's worse? I look over at you during lunch and there's not a mark on you." By this time, the two girls were out of the stall and standing in the open area in front of the sinks. "The way I see it, we're not done yet." Angie shoved Safia against the sink and gave her a powerful body shot to the gut, sending Safia to one knee gasping for air. "Ow!" Angie exclaimed, shaking her hand in pain.

"Leave her alone!" Sam yelled as she exited her stall.

"Stay out of this!" Angie yelled as she shoved Sam across the room. Turning her attention to Safia, Angie said, "I must have hit your belt buckle or something, but that's okay. I know how to fix all that." Angie smiled as she brought Safia back to her feet by the hair of her head and then slammed Safia's head into the sink, sending Safia's blood splattering onto the shiny, snowy-white surface of the hard porcelain. Safia grabbed her head in pain as she slid to the floor again.

"STOP!" Sam yelled as she stepped between Angie and Safia.

"You know what?" Angie thought aloud. "You're just as much a part of this as she is. So I'm gonna have to teach you a lesson, too."

Sam, knowing she is no fighter, embraced the inevitable and closed her eyes in anticipation of the terrible pain that was sure to come. Angie reared back her fist and threw a hard punch right at Sam's face. But instead of Sam's face, her fist ran into something that felt like a concrete wall as Safia caught the punch in midair. Angie let out a deep grunt of immense pain as Safia said, "No."

Safia threw Angie's fist back at her, and Angie doubled over in pain as she cradled her hand in her belly. Angie, through her laborious breathing, managed to whisper, "That's both my hands." Then, she yelled, "That's both my hands! What are you, some kind of freak?" And having said that, Angie quickly retreated from the bathroom.

Sam stood to her feet as she watched the bathroom door close behind Angry Angie. "Saf, you okay?"

"Yeah, I'm fine," Safia said, disgusted with the series of events that had unfolded throughout the day.

"Oh, my... my..." Sam whispered in disbelief, mouth agape, as she looked at Safia's forehead. "Safia... your forehead!"

"It doesn't really hurt that bad," Safia answered. "How does it look?"

Sam watched as the huge gash, at least two inches long, began to close right before her eyes. "You need to see for yourself. Quick. Look"

Sam gestured for Safia to turn and face the mirror. As Safia did, they watched in the mirror as the gash finished closing and became a thin, red line. The two girls leaned into the mirror together as they beheld the wonder of it all, the thin red line turning brown, then pink, then its normal dark, ebony color. "Did you see that, too?" Safia asked.

"Yeah," Sam whispered as they turned to face each other. "Instant healing. Not even a scar."

Suddenly, the door of the bathroom burst open and in walked Principal Waters. "What is going on in here, girls?" she demanded.

Safia was stunned, once again speechless. Sam, a little more resilient in high-pressure situations, managed to come up with, "Uh... Angie was in here and... she was very angry about something... like usual, right? Anyway... she was so mad... that she... punched the wall. Yeah, you should have seen it. It was like... whoa... what is she doing? You know?" Safia nodded her head and agreed. Sam continued, "I don't know WHO or WHAT set her off, but... she's pretty mad about something. But at least she didn't take it out on anyone else this time... right?"

"Well, are you two okay?" Principal Waters asked, buying the whole story.

"Uh, yeah," Sam replied. "Uhm, she didn't... she didn't mess with us at all. We were lucky, I guess. Right, Saf?"

Safia quickly agreed, "Right. I mean... she's kinda scary, you know. I'm glad I was in the stall. I just... hid in there, you know? But... now, I REALLY have to pee... so, can I?"

"Yeah, go ahead. And then get to class." Principal Waters lingered as both girls entered the stalls. She called over the doors, "So you're sure she didn't mess with either one of you?"

"Yes, Ma'am. We're sure," called Sam.

"Safia? Are you sure?" Principal Waters called out.

"Yes, Ma'am. I'm sure."

"Okay, then," Principal Waters called back. "I just needed to know before I call Angie's parents. Try to have a good rest of your day."

"You, too," both girls called back as Principal Waters made her exit, never noticing the blood on the sink.

Sam exited the stall and, when she went to wash her hands, she saw the blood. She grabbed a handful of paper towels and made sure to clean up all the blood before anyone else walked in and saw it.

Safia exited her stall and made her way to the sink to wash her hands as well. "That was too close," Safia muttered.

"Yeah. For real. Too close." They dried their hands and hurried back to class in an attempt to finish the day as if nothing had ever happened. As they scurried down the hallway, Safia realized that her new life of hiding her superpowers and trying to pass as normal wasn't off to the best start. And it wasn't even lunch yet.

"Hey, Chief," Lamar Henry called as he knocked on the open door of the fire chief's office. "You got a delivery you need to sign for."

"Tell 'em to come on in," Daniel Douglas answered. Just as the engineer was about to leave, the chief stopped him. "Hey, Lamar. Did you check the fuel on fifty-two?"

Lamar Henry spun around as he continued exiting and replied, "Topped it off an hour ago. Thanks for the heads up."

"No problem," he responded. Looking up at the delivery guy, Daniel Douglas motioned with his hand as he welcomed him with, "Come on in. You got somethin' for me?"

"Yes, sir. If you'll just sign right here." Jacob Tyler Mathew held out the clip board. Daniel began to reach for the pen in his pocket. "Got one already ready for you," Mathew quickly inserted as he handed the special pen to Daniel Douglas.

"Oh, thanks," Daniel said as he took the pen and signed his name on the dotted line. "Anything else?"

Mathew took the pen by the end and slid it into his shirt pocket, as if this were a ritual he had performed a thousand times. "No, sir. That should do it," he said as he handed the package to the chief. "You have a good day, sir." Mathew hurried off, comfortable with the fact that it didn't make him look suspicious, but rather, it made him look like he was in a prudent rush to get to his next delivery. Once outside the station, Mathew hummed a little tune as he hurried all the more to the delivery truck he was using and left the scene without stirring any suspicion at all.

Back inside the fire station, Daniel looked at the little package as he reached for a knife with which to open it. Just as he put the knife through the packaging tape, he froze. A little bit of healthy paranoia took him over, and he pondered the possibility that this might not be your typical package. He carefully pulled the knife out and turned the package over to examine the label. He was relieved when he saw that the sender was Fire Marshall Jason Briggsley. No doubt this was a sample of some new fire suppression control system or a new smoke detector that the department might endorse. Daniel laughed at himself for overreacting, for thinking for a moment that everything was bad news or danger. He turned the box back over and continued to use the knife to cut through the packaging tape. He opened the box and immediately threw it away as it exploded in a brilliant flash of light. He yelled out in fear and pain as the flash of fire came and went in an instant, eliciting a frenzied response from the firemen who ran to his aid.

"Are you alright, Chief?" asked Lamar Henry, who was first to enter.

"Yeah… I think… I think I'm alright." Daniel opened his eyes and blinked several times before confessing, "My eyes hurt real bad. Wow. And I got a ringin' in my head somethin' fierce." He looked up at his comrades who were now filling the room, one of them with the remains of the package in a shovel on the way out the door, just in case there was more to come. Daniel looked up at Joe Knight, the other engineer, who was now taking a look at the burns on his face and arm. "How bad is it?" Daniel asked as the realization of what had just happened began to sink in.

"Not too bad," Joe answered. "I think you're gonna be just fine." he added as he opened up the first aid kit that someone had just handed him. "What exactly happened?"

"That package that was just delivered… I looked at the label first. I thought it was safe, so I opened it. I saw the flash bomb activate as I was opening the inside flap and I managed to throw it away from me as it went off."

"Well… you're lucky. These burns appear to be superficial. Nothing above first degree. Singed your arm hairs for sure. But nothin' too bad. How about your eyes? How are they working?"

"Well... they hurt less, but... it's a little difficult to see with them right now."

"Then keep them closed until we can get a medicated eyewash kit. Then, we'll rinse those eyes real good and take you to the ER."

"I don't want to go to the ER. I'm sure I'll be just fine in a few minutes." Daniel Douglas could be stubborn as a mule in regards to his own health.

"Well, you may not WANT to go the ER, but our fire chief has this policy... and anyone injured on the job has to submit to the recommendation of the fireman who provides initial response treatment... that would be me... and I say that you're headed to the ER to have these burns and those eyes checked out... you know, just in case. Probably gonna check your ears to make sure there wasn't any damage to your hearing, too."

"Yeah, I seem to remember making that policy," Daniel conceded.

"Hey, Chief!" called Fire Captain Clay Charles. Take a look at what we found in the bottom of the box." He held out a metal plate with some lettering amateurishly burnt into the face which read, 'The Firefly Bandits.' Chief Douglas squinted a little as his eyes began to work a little better and he beheld the words burnt into the thin metal plate. He displayed a look of anger and disgust as he read the words. "Don't worry, Chief. We're gonna nail these bums and add attempted murder of a Fire Chief to their charges."

"I'm not worried," Daniel Douglas responded as he closed his eyes again. "I'm angry. I'm really, really angry... like I haven't been in a long time." Everyone looked on, not sure what else to say. The chief allowed his anger to subside as he concluded, "But for now, I need to call my wife and let her know what happened before she finds out from someone else... and I guess someone had better get me to the ER." Daniel reached for his cell phone, but only managed to grip it in his hand as the eye wash kit arrived and he had to surrender to his comrades as they began flushing his eyes.

"Okay, class, ten more minutes. I need you to work just ten more minutes on your assignment. It's not three o'clock for ten more minutes, so I'd better not see anyone putting their things away early. Jennifer, I swear to God, if you start putting your books up before... two fifty-eight... two fifty-eight, just work until two fifty-eight... because if you don't, I swear, I will ring your neck like a chicken's until you are dead and I'll record it and send it to your mom so she can get a laugh out of it, too."

The whole class giggled, and Jennifer's face erupted with a smile as she replied, "Yes, Ma'am." Mrs. Thompson was a veteran teacher who knew how to use humor to reach her students, and they all loved her, even when she was making outlandish threats to get her point across.

Suddenly, there came an announcement over the intercom in the room, "Mrs. Thompson?"

"Yes?" she answered with her head tilted up as if she were talking to God.

"I need Safia Douglas to come to the front office for pick up."

"Yes, Ma'am." she answered. Then, she looked at Safia and said, "Safia, you heard the lady. Get out of here before they change their minds."

The class let out a little giggle as Safia began to collect her things and replied, "Yes, Ma'am."

"Saf, why you gettin' picked up early?" Sam asked.

"I don't know," she replied as she stood up and started out of the room.

As she approached the front office, her mother rushed to meet her. "Come on, Babydoll," Jerrica said, taking some of her things from her.

"Mom, what's going on?" Safia asked, noticing the disturbed look on her mother's face.

"Just get in the car and I'll explain."

The moment the doors of the car were shut, Safia asked, "Okay, Mom, tell me. What's wrong?"

Jerrica quickly put the car in drive and started driving. "Your dad's okay, he expects to make a complete recovery, but... he's at the ER. There was an accident."

"Accident? What kind of accident?" Safia demanded.

"I don't know all the details just yet, but your dad is alert and he's in good spirits and... and he called me... so I spoke to him myself. He didn't even want to go to the ER, but he had to. But... the problem is..." Jerrica thought for a moment before she said, "Well... I'll have to let your dad tell you the rest... but he's fine, Babydoll, he's perfectly fine. He just has a few minor, MINOR... first-degree burns, that's all. He's okay. I assure you... he's okay."

"If he's okay," Safia asked, "then why are you doing sixty-five in a thirty-five?"

"Holy crap!" Jerrica exclaimed as she hit the brake pedal and slowed to a more reasonable speed.

"Just like you wanted, Boss," said Mathew as he carefully handed the pen to Zuri Walker. "Now... you, uh... you gonna let me in on what's goin' on with this guy and this pen?"

"Mr. Mathew, the less I tell you, the better. Just know this: I have a reason behind everything I do." Zuri Walker, latex gloves on her hands, took the pen from Jacob Tyler Mathew and began disassembling the pen. Once it was open, she tilted the larger, barrel portion to one side and a small device slid gently out of the barrel and into her palm. She held it up and looked at it closely before releasing a big, closed-lip smile. Then, she placed the tiny device into a receptacle that was connected to her computer. "The flash bomb served two purposes," she explained as she went to work on the computer. "First, it was to test our fire chief to see how fast his reflexes are... to see how quickly he heals..." she added with a sadistic grin, "... and to see how smart, or not smart, he really is. Second, and most importantly, it was a distraction... so that no one would think anything of the courier or the pen or anything like that. Their total attention will be on the contents of the box and who they believe sent it. Meanwhile, I am free to do my research both unsuspected and uninterrupted."

"But did you really have to put that flash bomb in that package?"

"Oh, don't be ridiculous," she defended herself as she continued to work on the computer. "I carefully chose and measured the ingredients myself so that he would only get a little burn. It made a big flash, but not a hot flash. Hmph," she laughed at herself as she realized she had inadvertently made a pun. "I assure you, he received minor burns, first degree at worst."

Mathew studied the computer monitor, totally clueless concerning the meaning of those things he saw on the screen. "I still don't understand what you want with this guy. I mean, what exactly are you lookin' for?"

"A hero, Mr. Mathew. I'm looking for a hero." She typed the last command and watched as the screen showed that the computer was running a long process, analyzing the data. She leaned back into her chair and tried to relax as she continued, "Like Bonnie Tyler. I need a hero."

The curtain was pulled back as Safia and Jerrica were led into the tiny station where Daniel sat on the hospital bed, waiting for the nurse to come back. "Oh, Baby," Jerrica said as she reached for him only halfway, not sure where or how she should or should not touch him. Safia was also anxious to hug her dad but unsure of what to do.

Daniel reached out his arms and said, "Come here, you two." His ladies came closer as he wrapped his bandaged arms around them. "Now, listen, both of you. I'm going to be perfectly fine. The doctors said that the burns aren't bad at all and that I shouldn't see any scarring in the long run. They figure a few weeks in bandages with the right medicine and lotions, and I'll be just fine. They were more worried about my vision and hearing, to be honest… WHICH," he interjected in an attempt to preempt further emotional fallout, "… they say is perfectly fine as well."

"Dad," Safia asked, "what exactly happened?"

Daniel looked at Jerrica for reassurance as he explained, "Well, Babydoll, it seems the Firely Bandits don't want me on their case, so… they sent me a little gift… thinking it would deter me from pursuing them any further. But it has had the opposite effect. Now, I'm more determined than ever to get them and, when I do, I'm gonna add assault of a government employee while on duty to the laundry list of charges against them."

"Can't you get them for attempted murder of a government employee?" Jerrica asked.

"Well, no, I don't think so. See, Phillip is already down at the crime lab assisting forensics and… they found that the substance used to make the flash bomb was the kind you use for stunts and shows… very little of the powder used in that bomb burns at a high temperature. So, basically… the bomb was not designed to kill… just to hurt and scare someone. But, if the DA wants to go after them for attempted murder, I won't argue."

"Well, this DA wants to go for attempted murder!" Jerrica responded.

"Hey, hey, something tells me you wouldn't be allowed on that case, Baby," Daniel replied with a little laughter.

"Maybe not, but I'm good friends with just about everyone in the DA's

Office, and I can assure you that they'll all be receiving an ample supply of encouragement from me to pursue the most aggressive charges possible."

Suddenly, their conversation was put on hold as the voices from behind the curtain a few stations over exploded. "What? No! THAT'S A LIE!"

"ARE YOU CALLING THESE DOCTORS LIARS? ARE YOU? LISTEN TO YOURSELF, ANGIE! YOU CAN'T EVEN TELL THE TRUTH ANYMORE!"

"BUT DOUG, YOU GOTTA BELIEVE ME! I DIDN'T PUNCH THE WALLS! I WAS IN A FIGHT!"

"AND YOU THINK THAT'S BETTER?"

"NO, BUT IT'S THE TRUTH!"

There was a moment of silence during which the Douglas family looked at one another, unsure of how to react to this awkward, uncomfortable moment. Safia tried to hide her emotions as the guilt began to set in as the father's voice asked, "Doctor, just tell me this. Is there a chance that the damage done to my stepdaughter's hands could have come from punching someone else?"

"Mr. McKinney, I'm not ruling anything out. But, I am saying that, after more than twenty-five years of medical practice with more than fifteen of those specializing in treating hand trauma, it is my professional opinion that your stepdaughter's injuries are consistent with those that I have seen countless times in cases where the patient got mad and punched a brick or concrete wall. The right hand? Maybe not. But the left hand? I cannot think of any other rational explanation for the trauma to the left hand. I'm sorry. Angie, I'm sorry. Now, we're going to get the swelling down first and then in a few days, maybe a week, we'll do some more x-rays and schedule surgery. Until then, ice, elevation, and rest are your new best friends. Mr. McKinney, can I speak to you outside for a moment?"

"Wow!" Jerrica whispered. "Do you know that girl, Babydoll?"

"Yes, Ma'am."

"Do you know what happened to her hands?"

Safia didn't like being dishonest with her parents. But she also knew that she could not tell them the truth. So she looked for a way to tell the truth and not tell the truth at the same time. "Well, Sam and I were in the bathroom when it happened. But we were in the stalls when she came in, so… I didn't actually see her hit the wall. But we both saw her leave, screaming, holding her hands to herself." Safia felt terribly dirty and disgusted with herself for not being forthcoming with the truth… but she was afraid.

"Wow!" Jerrica whispered again. "I'm so sorry you and Sam had to experience that."

"Yeah," added Daniel, "and I'm so glad she didn't hurt the two of you."

Safia felt even worse after hearing these things. All she knew to do was respond, "We're fine. I'm more worried about her than us."

Jerrica kissed Safia's forehead and gave her a big, approving hug as she exclaimed in a whisper, "That's my girl!" This only made Safia feel even lower than she did before. She had never lied about anything like this to her parents before, and the more her guilt mounted, the more her parents' pride in her made it painfully increase.

Safia sat in her secret circle of friends in the secret meeting place, having recounted the details of the day's events, including what she overheard at the ER.

Sam held her hand as she shared the last detail with the boys. "So, that's why Safia wants our help."

"Yeah, okay. Sure, Saf," Kenji answered. "What do you need?"

"Yeah… what he said," David added. "Whatever you need us to do, we're there for you."

Safia looked up into their eyes and declared, "I want you to help me learn how to control my powers."

"So you can be a superhero, right?" David cluelessly asked.

"So I won't hurt anyone else!" Safia answered sharply. "I'm no superhero. So far, I've managed to hurt Angie Dunlifsky so badly that she needs surgery… on BOTH HANDS… I got Jimmy Willis in trouble for lying when I was the one lying… not to mention, he knows the truth, so there's THAT problem I don't know what to do about…"

Sheepishly, Sam corrected, "It's 'that problem about which…'"

"I know! I know!" Safia interrupted. "I passed the test today, so it doesn't matter."

"Sorry. My fault."

"And on top of all that… I'm keeping secrets from my parents… and lying to them… or, at least it feels a lot like lying. I can't keep doing this."

"So… what are you getting at, Safia?" inquired Kenji.

"I don't want these powers. I don't want to have to worry about hurting someone. I don't want to have to cover up what's going on in my life, constantly worrying that another Jimmy Willis is gonna come along and tell everyone. Most of all, I don't want to lie to my parents or... or have to hide things from them. I don't want these powers. And I certainly don't want to be a superhero. So I need you guys to help me learn how to control my powers... so I never have to use them. I just want to be a normal girl again."

CHAPTER FOUR

⟨∞⟩

A HERO IS BORN

[Kilwa region of East Africa, 1752]

Bakari lay on the ground, bleeding profusely from the spear wound. The leader of the Adui attackers, General Kamili, surveyed the wreckage of Sirclantis's ship, unsure of what exactly this object was. One of the other warriors threatened Bakari further with his spear. General Kamili scolded, "No! It is obvious that he is familiar with the creature and this object. We may need him to answer questions." Looking down at Bakari, he added, "The Lekumba will die... just not yet." Kamili began rummaging through the cockpit of the ship, trying to make some sense of the truly alien things which he beheld. As he pressed on a certain panel of light, the entire cockpit lit up, startling him. A voice began to speak out of the control panel in Sirclantis's language. The voice sounded like a growl to the Adui, and they held up their spears in defensive positions, thinking that, perhaps, another stranger was about to attack. Finally, they realized that there was no danger, that the vessel was speaking to them. Kamili and his fellow Adui smiled and began laughing. "It speaks!" Kamili proclaimed in amazement. He walked over to Bakari and held the spear to Bakari's throat. "Tell me how it works, Lekumba."

Bakari gasped for air and reached deep down for enough strength to answer, "I do not know how it works. But even if I did, I would not explain such wonders to swine."

Kamili pulled the spear back and swung it, striking Bakari's face with the flat side of the spear head, sending Bakari all the way to the ground. "This swine was going to spare your life for a while. But I believe you. I believe that you do not know how to make this thing work. Which means I have no further use of you." Kamili nodded to his fellow Adui as he commanded them, "Stand him up!" The other Adui roughly took Bakari by the arms, one on each side of him, and forced him to his feet, holding him up in the absence of his own strength. General Kamili repositioned the sharp, deadly Adui spear in his hand in preparation for an execution. Before he ended Bakari's life, Kamili said to him, "Look upon me, Lekumba, and know this day that your life was ended at the hands of an Adui warrior." Kamili reared back the spear in preparation of a powerful thrust, preparing to run Bakari through with the weapon. But as he began to thrust forward with all his might, the spear was moved upon by some invisible force. Kamili could not make the spear move forward. Suddenly, the unseen force ripped the spear from Kamili's grip, and the spear flew swiftly through the air into the open palm of Sirclantis, who was reaching out of the regeneration capsule as the lid was still settling into its fully open position. Sirclantis, now fully healed of his wounds, climbed out of the capsule, and he stood fully erect upon his feet, a terrifying and awe-inspiring sight. He growled at the Adui and promptly broke the spear across his knee before assertively throwing the splintered remains of the spear aside.

General Kamili looked at his warriors as they took a step backward in fear. Kamili stirred himself and shouted, "What are you doing, cowards? We are three Adui warriors and it is but one. Flank me on either side and think of it as a lion." Then, with a wild, warrior smile, Kamili gave the order, "Let's go hunting." With a battle cry that rang through the dark African night, General Kamili led his warriors in the attack.

Sirclantis held his hand backward toward the cockpit of the ship, summoning his weapon, which flew through the air and made a loud smacking noise when it joined the palm of his right hand. The Adui attack came on all sides, the fierce warriors attacking in a pattern that they knew all too well, experts in combat. Sirclantis used his two-bladed weapon to block the first few attacks before deciding to defend himself with lethal force. He leapt through the air, performing a complete three hundred sixty-degree flip and slaughtering two of the Adui warriors in the process, and landed firmly on his feet before putting the weapon through the chest of General Kamili. Sirclantis forcefully pulled the weapon away, allowing the General's body to fall to the ground. Sirclantis's counterattack had lasted only three seconds. He looked around, still in battle posture, and saw a lone Adui warrior in the distance, and then watched the Adui warrior turn and run away. Then, he laid his weapon on the ground next to Bakari and beheld his wounds. Bakari was now barely conscious, the loss of blood too much for him to bear. Sirclantis spoke in his low, growling voice, and the device on his chest translated for him, "You should have run away and let me be. Why did you stay and fight?"

Bakari managed to whisper, "I don't know. I just thought it was the right thing to do."

Sirclantis picked up Bakari's head and held it in his immense hand. He watched as Bakari's eyes closed and a tear trickled down the face of this visitor from the stars. Sirclantis grumbled and the device on his chest translated, "Thank you. You saved my life." He took Bakari's body up in his arms and laid it on the wing of the ship before stepping back to consider the sacrifice which this complete stranger had just made for him. Overcome with emotion, Sirclantis grunted loudly, and as he took Bakari's body up in his arms again, the device on his chest translated, "No." He hurried over to the regeneration chamber and quickly placed Bakari's body inside. As he touched the panels, the chamber lit up again with its brilliant lights and an internal panel began showing wavy lines. Sirclantis spoke as he went to work and the device translated, "Good. You're still alive. I don't know if this will work, my new friend. But it's worth a try." The lid of the regeneration capsule began to close as Sirclantis held out his hand, summoning his weapon again. Taking guard he said, "You protected me while my life was in the balance. Now, I will protect you."

[Modern-Day Atlanta, Georgia, U.S.A.] Tuesday morning had arrived at Tweed-Johnson High School, and Safia Douglas timidly made her way into the school with her friends. A few students gave her strange, lingering looks, but most payed her no attention whatsoever. "I don't understand,"

Safia puzzled. "I was sure that I'd be all over social media by now, pictures or no pictures."

"Well," explained Samantha Castillo, "I don't think there's anything on social media about you. Some hacker genius must have planted a bug in the major social media servers that detected anything related to yesterday's events and erased them."

"People can do that?" David asked in amazement.

"No. PEOPLE can't do that. But I can," clarified Sam.

"Sam, that's not possible," disagreed Kenji. "There's no way that can be done, to plant a 'bug,' as you call it, in every major social media server without the various security measures detecting and rejecting it."

"Are you calling me a liar?" Sam fired back with a little attitude.

"No, I'm not saying you didn't attempt to do it. I'm just saying that there's no way to do it. Either you didn't get it all, or you got detected and someone's busting down your door any minute now looking for you. But there's no way to do what you said you did and get away with it."

"Well, I'll have you know that I can do what no one else can do. I know I'm normally modest, but…" Sam changed to a whisper as they started down the hallway, "…the truth is that I do all my usual hacking with basic ideas everyone else uses because I don't want to show what I can really do when people are looking. I'd end up in a federal prison if they knew what I can really do. So, yeah. I did just what I said I did. If I'm honest, I'm probably one of the best hackers in the world."

"Okay, stop the cap." Kenji returned. "There's no way that a tenth-grader from Atlanta, Georgia, is one of the best hackers in the world."

Sam responded, "Actually, I'm still being modest. I'm probably the best in the world."

Kenji replied, "Cap!"

Sam froze in her tracks for moment before turning and getting eye-to-eye with Kenji. They stared at each other awkwardly for several seconds, Kenji baffled by Sam's glare, until she announced, "Fine. Challenge accepted."

As she stepped back from him and reached into her bookbag for her laptop, Kenji said, "What challenge? I didn't challenge you to anything."

"Yes… yes you did," Sam explained as she opened her laptop and went to work. "You doubted my abilities… and my word. Well, I've got news for you. I grew up reading about coding and hacking and firewalls from the time I was a little girl. When other girls in Atlanta were reading princess stories, I was practicing my English by reading whatever my parents could find for me to read. They didn't want me to spend my whole life in the fields like them, and they knew that a command of the English language was one of the best chances I had. So you can imagine my joy when they brought home books that the library was giving away. They couldn't read English, so they didn't know what it was. But I had to read it anyway because it was all they had. So, when I was six, I didn't learn how to wait for a knight in shining armor to come to my rescue like other little girls. Instead, I learned how Jonathan James and Walter O'Brien hacked into NASA before they were sixteen. I was amazed that a couple of kids, each on their own, was able to do what grown-ups couldn't do and that no one thought possible. Of course, they were each caught and later would become ethical hackers, helping the government and other important entities protect their assets from digital intrusion. So, I was determined to do what they did. I studied everything I could find. My parents were so proud of my interest in computers that they scrimped and saved until they could buy me one. It was very basic, but I quickly learned how to upgrade it on my own. I started rebuilding my computer when I was eight, and I built a brand new one from scratch when I was nine. By the time I was ten, I was ready to join James and O'Brien... with one exception." At this point, Sam turned her laptop screen where her friends could see it. As they beheld the blueprints of the NASA rocket, she smiled and told them, "I never got caught."

Kenji read the descriptions and, as the realization came to him, he whispered, "Sam... that's the PR-22. They haven't even finished building it yet."

"I know. I just pulled this from NASA just now.... sitting right here in the floor of the hallway... and they have no clue."

"Sam, you shouldn't do this here!" Safia whispered in concern. "What about the cameras in the hallway?"

"Saf, I turned them off before I did this. What kind of amateur do you take me for?"

"Are you kidding me?" David whispered. "You can do that?"

Sam looked at David and blushed a little with pride that she had amazed him before bragging, "I have an IQ of 161 and my own personal library of digital and hard copy books spanning all of humanity's knowledge on the digital world. Plus, for the vast majority of my life, I've had time by the buckets. Plus, I really wanted to please my Papa and Mama. So, I became the world's best hacker. Or at least top two for sure. There's this one hacker, AQ52, that's probably ahead of me. But I'm sure I'll pass him pretty soon."

Kenji, blown away by the revelation, conceded, "Sam… I had no idea. I withdraw my previous criticism and… wow… put that away before someone sees it."

"Chill, bruh," Sam replied with a smile. "You really think anyone at this school has the first clue what this even is, even if they DO see it?"

"Facts!" David agreed.

"Yeah, you got a point there, I guess," Kenji said.

With the impact of the revelation setting in, Safia concluded, "So, that means that you were for real when you said that there's nothing on social media about me."

"For real as real can be," Sam reassured her.

"Wow. You really are the best friend ever," Safia praised.

"Well, you know," Sam responded with a smile.

"Okay, well, this has been… educational… for sure…" David said, "but I have first period class downstairs, and it's about that time, so… see you guys." His friends said their goodbyes to him as he left, and they started the other way down the hall. As they went, Sam looked back at David just in time to see him meet up with the scrawny kid from the day before. "You ready, kid?" he asked.

"I guess?" the scrawny kid replied.

"Don't worry. If there's any trouble, I'll distract them, and you run."

"That doesn't seem fair to you, man," the scrawny kid said.

"Nah. It's no big deal. I'm a faster healer than you, so… you know."

As they started down the stairs, Safia and Kenji paused to look back as well, hoping to hear no sounds of trouble emanating from the stair well. Theirs hopes were mercifully granted. Safia noticed the look on Sam's face, how she was so proud of David for taking care of the scrawny kid. "You can tell him how you feel, you know?"

"What?" Sam feigned. "I don't know what you mean. We're just friends, that all."

"Whatever," Kenji said as he walked away in disappointment.

"Safia, why would you say that?" Sam scolded. "Especially in front of Kenji?"

"But there's nothing to hide. We all know how you feel about him. Everybody, that is, except for David. You should tell him how you feel."

"No, I can't."

"But I saw how you were looking at him just now when he was helping that kid. We both did. Isn't that feeling that you felt when you saw him helping that poor kid worth telling him?"

"But what if he doesn't feel the same way about me?"

"Girl. Are you for real asking me that question?" Safia stopped and stared into Sam's eyes as she confessed, "Kenji and I have talked about it already. He's into you as much are you're into him. But neither one of you will make the first move. All I'm saying is that, sooner or later, one of you is going to have to make the first move."

"Well… then he'd better make the first move… because I don't think I can."

"So, let me get this straight," Safia examined her friend as she leaned in to whisper. "You're not afraid to hack NASA… repeatedly, apparently… but you're afraid to tell a great friend… who you know likes you… that you like him, too? Girl, you all kinds of messed up."

The two girls started walking again as Sam nodded her head in confirmation. "I know. I'm a chicken when it comes to boys."

"Well, then, man up, chicken," Safia said with a smile as the two girls entered the classroom.

"Deputy Director Simpson, please," Zuri Walker said into the telephone, staring with disappointment at the results of the tests she had run the day before. "Yes, Sir. This is Agent Walker. I have the test results from the target you assigned me. Not a match." Zuri listened to her boss's response before continuing, "Well, he did show possible carrier markers in his DNA, which means that we might be close. He could be related to someone who fits our profile. And get this: his daughter has a Swahili name." She smiled as she responded, "I know. I found that very interesting as well. So, although Daniel Douglas is not our guy, I think someone in his family just might be. With your permission, I'd like to expand my search to include his next of kin." She listened for a moment, nodding her head, and replied, "Yes, Deputy Director. I'm sure I can get what I need unnoticed." An irritated countenance took over her face for a moment as she replied, "Do you really want to know how I get my job done so quickly or do you just want results?" She huffed and puffed away from the receiver of the phone as she listened before replying, "With all due respect, Deputy Director, you assigned me to this task because I'm the best the agency has at tracking down super-powered individuals, and if the threat we're preparing for is real, we're going to need someone special to help us or we're basically sunk. So let me do my job, Sir." Zuri nodded her head in victory and said, "Yes, Sir. Thank you, Sir. I'll get it done." As Zuri Walker ended the call, she looked over at Jacob Tyler Mathew, who was eating a jelly donut, jelly running down the side of his mouth. She shook her head and said to him, "I carry a burden you will never have to bear. I have to work for someone whose intelligence is considerably lower than my own." A confused look appeared on Mathew's face as Zuri continued, "Don't worry about it, Mr. Mathew. You wouldn't understand, even if I spelled it out for you."

Mathew puzzled even harder before quickly and aggressively wiping the jelly from his mouth, thinking her words referred to his appearance. "Is that better, Ms. Walker?" he asked.

"Yes," Zuri said, slightly amused, slightly irritated. "That's better. You look smarter already."

The circle of friends sat down together at the lunchroom table, grateful that the menu for the day included lasagna. "Mmmm. This smells great!" Sam said. "The one thing the lunchroom gets right. Delicioso."

"So, I haven't had a chance to ask you, Safia," David said. "How has your day gone? Any problems?"

"Nope," Safia replied shortly, anxious to stuff her face with a steamy, yummy forkful of lasagna.

"How about you?" Sam asked David. "Did you and the skinny kid have any issues?"

"Nope," David replied, also anxious to stuff his face. He inserted the forkful of steamy, yummy lasagna into his mouth and savored its warm, cheesy, saucy, meaty heartiness. After chewing and swallowing, he continued, "No problems at all. And speaking of no problems at all, if anyone doesn't have an appetite for lasagna today and you have a problem figuring out what to do with your lasagna, you do not have a problem at all. I can hook you up. I'm your guy."

Kenji smiled and shook his head. Then he asked, "So, Safia... have you given any more thought to what you decided yesterday? I mean, so far, there haven't been any problems today. Jimmy Willis hasn't said anything else."

Safia responded, "Jimmy Willis isn't saying anything else because he got in trouble yesterday and can't prove anything. But he gave me a look this morning."

"What kind of look?" Kenji said with a protective, indignant demeanor.

"The kind of look that says, 'We both know you lied, and I'm mad you got me in trouble.' I'm afraid we haven't heard the end of Jimmy Willis."

"Well, first of all," Sam responded, "you wouldn't have had to lie if Jimmy Willis had just minded his own business. So, Jimmy Willis got HIMSELF in trouble because he's a nosy Ned. And second, if he so much as even THINKS about causing any more trouble for my BF, I'll hack his social media accounts and make him wish he was never born."

"Chill, girl!" Safia said. "I don't want him to go home and hang himself. I just want him to back off."

"Well, I could have a talk with him or something," Kenji said.

"What do you mean 'a talk'?" Safia asked.

"You know... a talk," Kenji replied.

"You mean... you're going to threaten him? Or you mean you're going to distract him? Or you mean you're going to what?" Safia demanded.

"I wouldn't call it a threat," Kenji answered. "Just... a talk between guys... you know... to make sure there is no misunderstanding."

"I don't think I like the sound of this," Safia scolded. "You're just going to make things worse. And besides, that not you. Or at least that's not the you I've known my whole life. And that's not the you I want you to become, so... why don't you just let me handle it. Okay?"

"Yeah. Sure," Kenji replied awkwardly. "I didn't mean to..."

"Just drop it," Safia commanded. At this point, Safia stood to her feet and said, "I need to get another napkin. I've got a lot more lasagna left and

I'm already out of napkin." She smiled, hoping her humor would break the tension.

As she walked away, Sam asked Kenji, "What is wrong with you? We're supposed to be the good guys. You know... nice people? We don't make threats, and... it sounded an awful lot like you were intending to threaten Jimmy Willis."

"Not cool, bruh," David added.

"Yeah, I know, but..." Kenji said, getting a little more emotional, "I don't know, I... I just got so mad thinking about how Safia is going to suffer if Jimmy goes unchecked. I mean, someone has got to do something before he ruins Safia's life, right?"

"Calm down, Kenji," Sam said. "You're not acting like yourself."

"Yeah, man," agreed David, "chill, bruh. This ain't you. You're always the realist, chillest guy in town. I've never seen you so out of control of your emotions like this before."

"What are you talking about?" Kenji defended himself. "I'm always passionate about the things I believe in and the people in my life. The real question is: why aren't you guys more upset than you are?"

Safia returned, a pile of napkins in her hand. "I'm back. Prepared for lasagna." She smiled and sensed the tension at the table. "Oooooooh-kayeeeee. I don't know what happened while I was gone, but whatever it is, let's just drop it, shall we?"

Suddenly, David's face exploded, his eyes bulging to the brink of popping out of his head. "Oh my!" he exclaimed.

"What? What is it?" Sam asked.

Everyone was looking at David as he pondered his next words and his next move. "Uhhh... uhhh... I... I don't have enough napkins either and... I'm ready to really tear into the rest of this lasagna. Hey, Saf. I'm stuck over here next to the wall. Do you think you could get ME some napkins, too?"

Safia chuckled, "I'm sure I have enough to share. You can have some of mine, you know?"

"I don't know. I'm real hungry and... everyone knows I'm a real messy eater." David looked at Safia and concluded, "I really need a stack of my own... like... twice as big as yours."

Safia looked at David, visibly confused, puzzling for the meaning of his behavior. "Uhm… sure, David… whatever. I'll… get you a BIG stack of napkins." She rose from the table and went back again to the napkin dispenser, feeling as though she had been dismissed for some secret meeting.

As soon as she left, Sam began to ask what was wrong. "David, what's…"

But before she could finish, David blurted out in a powerful whisper, "You're totally in love with Safia!"

Kenji fired back in his own powerful whisper, "What? That's ridiculous!"

"No!" David continued. "You are! And it makes total sense."

"It does?" Kenji replied. "Wait! What do you mean? I'm not in love with Safia!"

"Oh my God!" exclaimed Sam in an even louder whisper. "You ARE in love with her!"

"KEEP YOUR VOICE DOWN!" Kenji shouted in a whisper.

"So, it's true!" David said.

"I didn't say that!" Kenji defended.

"But you can't look me in the eyes and deny it, can you?" Sam asked. "Come on. Look me in the eyes and tell me you don't love her. Then I'll know for sure."

Kenji looked Sam directly in the eyes and said, "I don't… I mean… I don't know what…"

Safia suddenly sat down and threw the handful of napkins at David. She smiled as she noticed the looks on her friends' faces, the former tension gone, and whispered, "What are you guys whispering about?"

The other three friends froze, not sure how to answer. Then, Sam busted out giggling about the situation as Kenji blushed a little, and David was forced to come up with an answer. "Uh… there's too many people in here. Sam will have to tell you later." When he said this, Kenji's eyes widened, eliciting full-blown laughter from Sam. Soon, David joined the laughter.

Safia looked at Kenji, who was not laughing, and wondered what this could possibly mean. "Don't look at me," Kenji said. "I didn't get the joke." Looking at his other two friends he added, "I didn't find it funny at all."

"Well," replied Safia with an anxious smile, "if it's this funny, I can't wait to hear it later." When she said this, Kenji was overcome with fear, realizing that Safia would ask Sam later… and perhaps Sam would tell Safia about the conversation… and perhaps that made him nervous… because perhaps they were right.

As he pondered these things, an announcement came over the intercom system, "Attention all tenth-grade students. Attention all tenth-grade students. A representative from FTDVA will be here tomorrow to meet with you during an assembly seventh period. She will have information about colleges and scholarships for which you may qualify. These offers are available only to tenth-grade students and you must signify your interest tomorrow in order to be considered for one of their programs. It is very important that you attend tomorrow. Teachers, we will dismiss students for assembly immediately upon the seventh period tardy bell. Thank you for giving up your instructional time to make this opportunity for our students possible."

The lunchroom erupted in chatter. "Who is FTDVA?" asked Safia. "I've never heard of them."

"I don't know," replied Sam, "but maybe they have a program for computer science. If I could get a STEM scholarship for a good college, that would be totally awesome."

"Yeah, and maybe they know a way I can become a doctor and study music at the same time," David said. His friends looked at him with total surprise. "What?" he asked with a smile on his face.

"Since when do you want to be a doctor?" Kenji asked.

"Since I've never had a choice in the matter," David answered.

"What?" Sam asked. "I don't understand."

"Look. In my family, we're doctors. All of us. Whether we practice medicine or not, that doesn't matter. We're all doctors first. It's not even a choice."

"That's weird," Sam said.

"Well, that's the way it is in the Norris Family. Everyone has to study physiology from an early age. We're experts by requirement."

"Totally weird," Sam reiterated.

"Not as weird as you think," Kenji responded. "In my family, it doesn't matter what you want to do with your life, you're going to learn martial arts, especially swordsmanship. And it's not even a choice. So I totally get it."

"In my family, you're going to be an expert on Shujaa Nguvu and the A-Power comics, whether you want to be or not. I know that's not exactly the same thing, but... I get it. You have to do it because it's a family thing."

There was silence among the circle of friends for a moment. Then, Sam said, "Well, in my family it's the right opposite. The family business for two generations has been harvesting in the fields. My parents want me to do anything BUT what they did. So, I don't get it... personally... but I can see how different families have different priorities."

"Well... our three families are a little more different than others," responded David. "I guess that's why our parents are such close friends. They understand each other."

"Yeah, but I didn't realize that your family was... like... mandating that you be a doctor," Kenji said. "But if your family is anything like mine, that means that you're already well on your way to being an expert. Which would explain why you always make A's in Biology and Chemistry. So, just tell me. How much do you already know?"

"Well, I haven't told anyone... not even you, Kenji... but I'm actually dual enrolled and I have finished the first two years of college in pre-med."

"What?" exclaimed Safia with a smile.

"No way!" shouted Sam. "But you're only in tenth grade!"

Kenji smiled as he shook his head. "When did you even have time to do all this... and me not find out about it?"

"Well, I kinda don't let anyone know about it, but... I'm technically a genius."

Kenji laughed a little as he said, "Stop the cap, bruh."

"I'm not cappin', Kenji. One forty-five: that's my IQ."

"That certainly qualifies you as a genius," Sam answered with awe.

"And you would know, right?" redirected David.

"Uh, well... yeah, I mean... I guess," Sam responded awkwardly.

"You may come from a completely different kind of family from ours, but you're the smartest person at this table," Kenji explained. "You're the smartest person at this school. So you understand where David is coming from. Do you let EVERYONE know what you can do?"

Sam immediately responded, "No. I don't want everyone knowing what I can do."

"Exactly. You understand David more than anyone here," Kenji continued. "Which is why it would be totally cool if you and David ever wanted to have some time alone to talk nerd stuff."

Safia smiled and jumped on board, "Yeah, I mean... I wouldn't want to be in one of your conversations... whew, way over my head... but you guys should totally hang out sometime without us."

Realizing what Kenji and Safia were doing, David and Sam became uncomfortable. Kenji realized this, too, and quickly changed the subject, "Uh, David... you... gotta help me study for the next biology test, then, right?"

"Uh, yeah. Sure, man," David replied, realizing that Kenji was mercifully changing course.

"And Sam..." Safia added, "youuuuu caaaaaan... uhmmmm... help me..." Safia was rescued by the signal to return to class. Then, the most hilarious and awkward thing that could possibly happen took place as Safia grabbed her things and said, "I'll think of something you can help me with later. Let's go." The circle of friends departed the lunchroom, tension now between them in ways that had never been before.

"Hey, Chief?" called Fire Captain Clay Charles as he greeted Daniel Douglas. "Perfect timing. You have a phone call from the deputy fire marshal.

"Grant?" Daniel asked with enthusiasm.

"Yes, Sir, Chief."

"Thanks. I'll take it in my office." Fire Chief Daniel Douglas quickly fell into his office chair and picked up the phone, pressing the line button as he answered, "Hello, Phillip?"

On the other end of the line, Deputy Fire Mashal Phillip Grant, head of fire-related investigations, responded, "Hey, Daniel. We got a hit on facial recognition on one of the perps from the station arson. We're lookin' at a Wesley Nolan McGuiness, 2348 Doulan-Burgess Avenue Apartment 16-C, twenty-four years of age, one prior for petty theft, one prior for possession with intent. He's actually on probation right now, so County called his PO. He's gonna go around and pick him up for questioning. This is the big break we needed. He's already lookin' at a year for the petty theft and two years for the possession, plus twenty years for each count of arson, and his PO says he doesn't think this is the kinda guy who can do hard time, so he'll probably give up his buddies in a heartbeat."

"That's great news! I want names, addresses, everything on these other guys as soon..."

"Whoa, whoa, whoa, whoa," Phillip cautioned. "Let the police handle it. They've got this."

"That's not right! You expect me to sit back and do nothing while the boys in blue close in on our guys?"

"Yes, Fire Chief," Phillip emphasized. "That's exactly what I expect you to do! I expect you to abide by the law and let the police handle this! We've done our part and now it's in the hands of law enforcement. Let them do their job."

Daniel put his palm across his forehead and began to rub it to relieve the tension in his body. "You're right. I'm sorry. I don't know what came over me. It's just... these punks hit our fire station... MY fire station... and they made it personal with that flash bomb. I'd be lying if I said that it doesn't still burn... really bad... so, I really want these guys."

"Yeah, but... that's what they want. They want you to make it personal. The way to get two-bit punks like this? You just go about business as if it's just another day and they're just the latest in a long line of punks you deal with every day. Don't give 'em the satisfaction of knowing they got under your skin. 'Cause if you do, they win. Do you want them to win?"

The words he heard resonated within his being as a new resolve came over him. "No. I will not let these punks win. You help the police deal with the Firefly Bandits. I've got some safety checks I need to sign off on with some new equipment that arrived last week."

"That's the Daniel Douglas I know."

"It's just... I don't want them to feel like they won, you know?"

"They only win if they make you become someone you're not," Phillip Grant reminded his friend.

Daniel smiled as he replied, "Now, where in the world did you hear a thing like that?"

"From the wisest fire chief I ever met. You just be sure you practice what you preach. You hear?"

"Will do. And Phillip? Thanks. I really needed that."

A well-dressed black male knocked on the door of an apartment in a failing neighborhood. The door opened as far as the safety chain would allow as a ragged white female in her mid-twenties responded, "Yeah?"

"Hello, Ma'am. I'm Gerald Kennison. I need to speak to Wesley." She was hesitant to respond, just glaring at him. "I'm his probation officer."

The woman glared for a moment more before leaning back and yelling, "Wes! There's someone at the door for you!" Leaning back toward the opening of the door, she spoke through the crack, safety chain across the middle of her face, "He'll be here in a minute." The door then closed as Gerald Kennison waited. He looked around for a second, taking in the sounds of people yelling out the windows at each other as the wind-driven leaves danced across the pavement in a crinkling sound.

He heard the woman's voice through the walls of the apartment, "Wes, I swear to God, if you're in some kind of trouble…"

"I'm not in any trouble! What are you talking about?"

"It's your parole officer! He's at the door! You better not be in any trouble!"

"I'm clean as a whistle. I swear to God I am!" There came the sound of the chain being loosed, and the door opened as Wesley Nolan McGuiness stuck his head out of the door and said, "Mr. Kennison. Nice to see you. What can I do for you?"

"Get dressed. We're going to the precinct for a drug screen."

"Aww, you gotta be kidding me!" Wesley complained. "I just wizzed the cup last week!"

"Yeah, well… it's one of those random things, you know. But it shouldn't be any trouble. I mean… you're clean, right?"

"Yeah, I'm clean. I swear to God."

"Well, let's go prove it to everybody and I can bring you back and you can go back to doing whatever you were doing, right?"

"Yeah. But I gotta get dressed."

"Not a problem. Just let me inside and I'll accompany you. Gotta keep my eye on you, you know?"

"Yeah, yeah. I know the drill."

A few minutes later, Gerald Kennison and Wesley Nolan McGuiness were in the government-issue car headed to the precinct. "Here," Kennison said as he handed him a bottle of water. "It'll help you pee."

"That's okay," Wesley replied. "I've got my own. I don't know what's in that."

Kennison smiled with amusement as he said, "Okay, that's fine."

"I don't mean to be rude or anything like that," Wesley explained. "It's just that... you know what I mean? Police and all that. You can't trust cops these days."

"I understand," Kennison replied with a smile. "You don't have to explain yourself to me. If you don't want the water I'm offering, that's perfectly fine."

"Yeah, but... I don't mean that YOU are a dirty cop or nothin' like that... it's just... you know... it's hard for me to trust ANYBODY... so I'd rather be safe than sorry."

"It's okay. I'm okay. All I want is for you to pee clean today so we can both go back to what we were doing. That's all."

"Yeah. We'll see if that's all," Wesley responded with cynicism. Kennison chuckled with amusement as they continued down the street toward the precinct.

Zuri Walker's cell phone vibrated on the countertop. "Yes, Deputy Director Simpson." she answered with a little irritation noticeable in her voice. "Yes, Deputy Director, three thousand dollars." Ms. Walker was offended when someone questioned her expertise and wisdom in matters. "Look, Sir. When I analyze a situation and say that something is necessary, then it is necessary. So let me do my job, and you don't worry about how much it costs to do it right. Just trust that I always do it right." She listened as she rifled through a stack of paperwork, highlighting a few lines of information in key areas of concern. "Now that's the first thing you've said all day that's made any sense. After all, I wouldn't be doing this if we weren't staring down a credible threat. So let me do my job and find the help we need before we're caught unprepared at the most crucial moment in human history. You handle the red tape and the finances, and I'll orchestrate the return of the Mashujaa. Believe me, the Executive Director will be thanking us when the United States Department of Defense is responsible for saving the world. So, if you don't mind, I have work to do, Sir. Good-bye."

"Okay, what's going on, Ms. Walker?" Jacob Tyler Mathew asked. "And what's a mashugana got to do with anything?"

"Uhh!" Zuri Walker sighed with disbelief. "Not a mashugana. That's Yiddish for a crazy, nonsensical person. Mashujaa. It's Swahili. It means 'heroes.' Used in the proper context, it can refer to a team of superheroes working together for the common good."

"Wait. You mean you're trying to find superheroes? Huh. Lady, you gotta be crazy."

"Yeah, I'm a regular mashugana. I know. Just do your job and let me worry about all that other stuff." To herself she continued, "Really, I've got to find you a language tutor if I'm going to keep you around." She then spoke up a little as she addressed Mathew, "So, what have you found on our girl?"

"You mean Safia Douglas?"

"No, I mean Madonna. Yes, Safia Douglas, you twit. What have you found on her?"

"Okay, she's a tenth-grade student at Tweed-Johnson High School. She excels in math and history, mostly A's and B's in all her classes, some C's in English Language Arts last year. Hangs out with three other students all the time. Best friend is a Samantha Castillo Cruz, daughter of Eduardo Castillo Juarez and his wife Maria Cruz Sanchez, both harvesters at a nearby produce farm. Two guy friends, David Norris, son of Dr. Oliver Jacob Norris, M.D., and his wife Dr. Natalie Norris, D.N.P. and H.M.D."

"Norris, you say?"

"Yes, Ma'am. Norris."

"Both of them are doctors?"

"Yes, Ma'am."

"Interesting. Continue."

"Okay, they have a joint practice in Metro-Atlanta, husband is considered one of the best surgeons on the East Coast, wife is considered a health guru and specializes in non-traditional treatments. Other guy friend, Kenji Nakajima…"

"Nakajima?!" Zuri interrupted.

"Yeah, Nakajima. Father's name is Minato Nakajima, software bigwig, and mother is Akira Nakajima. Minato's father lives with them, name…"

"Kaito…" Zuri interrupted with perfect Japanese pronunciation and accent, a look of awe glazing her eyes. "Nakajima Kaito, once one of the greatest swordsmen in all of Japan and member of the secret society of the Nakajima family." As if remembering an old friend whom she admired greatly, she continued, "I thought he was dead."

"Well, he's very much alive. You know him?"

Zuri Walker didn't want to answer and so prompted Mathew with, "Anything else on the friends and their families?"

"Nothing of note. But you know these people already, right? I mean, we gotta be close to finding whoever you're looking for."

"Some of the names are right... some of the professions are right... I just don't know exactly how all these pieces fit together just yet, so I'm not sure what it is that we've found. I just know we've found something. But I'll know a lot more after tomorrow. In the meantime, I have a new assignment for you." Zuri Walker picked up a small collection of papers as she stood to her feet and walked over to Jacob Tyler Mathew and handed him the papers, one at a time, as she explained his instructions. "Take this to the public records office and ask for Jennifer Grant. Give this to Ms. Grant. She'll know what to do. Wait for her until she returns with an envelope. You'll bring that envelope to me when you are done with the other errands. When you leave public records, take this ticket to the address on it and pick up my dry cleaning."

Holding a stack of envelopes bundled with a rubber band, Mathew asked, "And what is this?"

"That would be my outgoing mail. Don't take the rubber band off. Don't look at any of it. Just drop it in the mail. Understand?"

"Yes, Ms. Walker."

"Good. Now, get stepping. I have work to do here, and I don't need you distracting me."

"Yes, Ma'am," he replied as he hurried off to perform his tasks.

As he departed, Zuri Walker whispered to herself, "Good help is so hard to find these days."

Safia nodded at Sam, trying to get her attention. Sam mouthed to her, "What?"

Safia cut her eyes over at Kenji and mouthed, "What's up with him?"

Sam, playing dumb, and trying to go unnoticed by Ms. Sawyer, mouthed back, "I don't know. He seems fine to me."

"What?" Safia mouthed back.

"He seems fine to me." Sam mouthed again.

"What?" Safia mouthed again.

"Ladies?" Ms. Sawyer interjected. The two girls' heads whipped around immediately in shock, their eyes open wide. "Is there anything you would like to share with the rest of the class?"

"Uhm, no, Ma'am," Safia replied.

"Is your communication related to inverse functions?" Ms. Sawyer asked.

"No, Ma'am," Sam responded.

"Then I suggest you wait until after class to have this discussion."

"Yes, Ma'am," they replied in unison. Safia looked over at Kenji, who had been looking at her during the exchange between the teacher and his friends. As soon as Safia's eyes met his, he quickly looked down at his schoolwork. Safia didn't like this very much and became even more suspicious of Kenji's behavior, although she was clueless regarding the true nature of his strange actions and demeanor. This was indeed a puzzle that kept her distracted.

At the end of class, the circle of friends met just outside the door of Ms. Sawyer's room as always. "We're headed on to the gym," said David. "And I'm gonna drain threes in Kenji's face today. Ain't that right, bro?"

"In your dreams," Kenji answered with a big smile. "Gotta go, ladies," he said to the girls. "He hit a few threes last week and he thinks he can play basketball now. It's my responsibility to humble him and bring him back to Earth before he shoots his mouth off and embarrasses himself."

"You? Humble me?" David fired back as they headed off to gym.

"Yeah, and don't take it personal, okay? I'm just being a friend."

Safia smiled a little as she watched them walk away, glad that a little bit of normal had returned. But then her thoughts drifted back to the awkward moments that had occurred first at lunch and then, again, in the classroom.

"So, what's with this inverse function stuff?" Sam asked.

"What do you mean?" Safia asked in response.

"I mean: who gets this stuff?"

"Look: it's easy. Whatever you would do to isolate the independent variable, that's what you now do to the independent variable and that's the inverse function. For example: if f of x equals two x plus six and you rewrote the equation isolating x, you would first subtract six and then divide by two. So, f inverse of x would be x minus six, quantity divided by two."

Sam just looked at Safia with her mouth agape, awe in her eyes. "Girl, are you for real?"

"Yeah, that's how you do it."

"No. I mean, I know how to do it. I get it. But nobody else in the room gets it. Except, obviously, for you. Girl, you rattled that off like a pro. You been holdin' back on me?"

"What do you mean?" Safia replied with a little confusion.

"I mean, I'm a genius and I understand advanced algebra just fine. But girl, you just spittin' that out there like a textbook or somethin', like it's no big deal."

"But it's really not that big a deal."

"Uh, yeah. It is. Tell me: what kind of grades do you get in math?"

"A's. But lots of people get A's in math."

"Not really," Sam fired back with sarcasm. "Okay, what's the quadratic formula?"

"Oh, come on, Sam."

"Shhp! Shhp! Shhp!" Sam said in an excited, irritated, manner. "Quadratic formula!"

Safia sighed before blurting out, "Opposite b plus or minus the square root of b-squared minus four A C all over two A."

"How was it derived?"

"Someone started with the quadratic equation and completed the square."

"What's the slope of the function f of x equals three x plus 4?"

"Three over one, okay?"

"What's the slope of the function y equals negative 3?"

"Zero?" Safia replied as if confused by an elementary question.

"What's the slope of the function x equals 4?" Sam asked with ever-increasing excitement.

"Undefined! Okay? And it's not a function!"

"What's the sine of forty-five degrees?" Sam exploded.

"I don't know! Radical two over two maybe? I haven't taken trig yet."

"OMG, SAF! WHAT'S TWENTY-THREE TIMES FIFTY-TWO?"

"Uhm… uhm… uh… one thousand one hundred…" Safia looked upward as she made her final calculation, "ninety-six!" The two girls just looked at each other. Safia, now a little excited, asked, "Is that right?"

Sam exclaimed, "I don't know. I'm a genius, not a human calculator." She quickly pulled out her cell phone and put in the calculation to discover that Safia was indeed right. She held the phone up and turned it around so Safia could see the answer: one thousand one hundred ninety-six.

"I've… always been good at math… that's all," Safia responded sheepishly, realizing that several friends had stopped to watch the exchange.

Sam, realizing that the attention was unwanted, moved in and grabbed Safia by the hand and led her away. As they left, Ms. Sawyer leaned out the door of her room and smiled with amazement, nodding her head in approval as she tucked away the new information in a safe spot in her mind until called upon.

"Saf, you're mathematically gifted, girl!" Sam whispered loudly as they journeyed down the hallway to toward the gymnasium. "That's why you've always been good at math."

"You really think so?"

"I know so. And I'm a genius, so don't argue with me about this stuff."

"Wow," Safia whispered to herself in amazement. "I'm not sure how I feel about this."

"Well, I'm jealous. I mean, I'm really good at math and stuff, but that human calculator stuff is next level for me."

"Well, me and math are… friends… I guess," Safia concluded, trying to minimize the gravity of the situation.

"Well, me and math aren't always on the best of terms, if you know what I mean."

"But you're so good at math," Safia puzzled.

"Algebra and statistics? Yeah. Linear and quadratic functions? Yeah. You kinda have to be good at that stuff for programming because there's a lot of function language and Bayesian probability in coding. But those calculations? Girl! Impressive!"

"Shhh!" Safia demanded as they entered the gym. "Zip it! I don't want to have this talk in front of everyone else."

"Okay. I understand," Sam responded. After a few seconds, Sam whispered, "What's the vertex of the function f of x equals two x squared plus eight x plus 7."

"Sam!" Safia fired back in a powerful whisper.

"Sorry," Sam replied.

A few seconds later, Safia, in spite of herself, whispered back, "Negative two, negative one."

"Hehehe," Sam giggled as she whispered. "You're totally a nerd, now. Welcome to the outcasts of society."

"Oh, hush!" Safia whispered back as they entered the girls' locker room on the far end of the gymnasium.

"Okay, you're clean!" Kennison called out to McGuiness.

"I know. I told you I was clean!" McGuiness fired back.

"Well, in my line of business you never can tell until you get the test results back. But, for what it's worth, I was really bettin' on you. Give us just a few minutes to finish with the paperwork and then I'll take you home."

"Okay. But hurry up. It's my day off and I'm ready to be at the house."

Kennison smiled and nodded as he turned to walk away. But at that moment, another officer looked at him and gave him a nod. Kennison nodded back and then turned and walked over to McGuiness. Putting his hand on his shoulder, Kennison said, "Wes… I need you to come with me. We need your help with a case we're workin' on, and I told my colleagues that you would be glad to lend a helping hand. Right?"

Confused and skeptical, Wesley McGuiness responded, "I guess, yeah. What's this about?"

A few minutes later, Kennison was looking over the notes from the questioning as he asked, "So as soon as I walked out and you walked in…"

"He sang like a canary," Terry Tolliver said. "All I did was flex this twenty-two-inch upper arm 'til it made the seams of my shirt scream when I handed him the bottle of water… he took one look at my face… then he said, 'What do you want to know?' You called it right. He's terrified of police."

"And these names?"

"We're already running them through the database. We should have a warrant for their arrests within the hour, assuming the software can match them."

"It will. I'm sure of it," Kennison confidently declared.

"Well, I'll call Grant over at the Fire Department and let him know what's happening," Tolliver said. "They could use some good news right about now. Thanks for your help, Gerald."

"My pleasure, Terry. Uhm, tell me: you gonna hold McGuiness here or do I have to escort him somewhere else?"

"Nah, I'm pretty sure we've got 'em now. You're good to go. I'll call you if I need anything else," Tolliver said as he extended his hand.

Kennison took his hand in a firm grip as he replied, "Pleasure doing business with ya', Terry."

"Likewise," Tolliver responded in turn. As he watched Kennison walk out of his office, he chuckled a little as he whispered to himself, "That was too easy." Then, he got a funny feeling as he whispered to himself again, "That was too easy." But he convinced himself to shake to uneasy feeling and embrace the reality that they had finally caught the Firefly Bandits and that soon there would be warrants and arrests, and that would be the end of it all.

During gym class, the girls were playing half-court basketball on one end of the court and the boys were playing half-court on the other end. Safia was playing shooting guard, mainly because of her undersized stature and a little because of her ball-handling skills. On the other end of the floor, David and Kenji again found themselves on opposing teams. Every time David would get the ball, Kenji would switch with his teammate and guard David. Kenji was using his slightly taller stature and lean physique to beat David with quickness. Safia watched for a moment as her two best guy-friends went at it.

"Safia!" she heard as she turned her head just in time to see the ball coming her way. She immediately jumped back into action on the girls' end of the court and made a quick dribble and sidestep motion before putting up an outside jump-shot.

The ball rattled in and out of the rim, cascading down toward the hands of the many girls fighting for the rebound. Her teammate, Cindy, got the put-back goal, eliciting an eruption of praise and cheers from her teammates. "You'd better be glad Angie isn't out here!" shouted one of the girls on the other team. "You know she eats boards for breakfast, lunch, and snack." Suddenly, Safia was not so gleeful. She turned and scanned the sidelines until she located Angie. There she was sitting on the bottom row of the bleachers, both hands bandaged. Safia thought about the bandages that she had worn for the last few days and how they had hidden her healing. But these bandages were hiding the severity of the damage that was nowhere near healing. Angie hadn't even had surgery yet. Safia quickly went back to the game as her friends called to her, but all throughout the remainder of gym class, all Safia could think about was Angie.

By the end of gym class, Safia had only scored seven points. She usually averaged twelve points in actual games, but her heart just wasn't into it today. She looked down at the boys' end of the court to see Kenji patting David on the head as they exited the court. "How many points?" Kenji called out obnoxiously. "How many?"

David, a smile on his face, muttered, "Four."

"Four? Four you say? Boy, I score four at my own funeral. And that's with the casket already closed and sealed. And how many threes did you hit today?"

Still sporting a smile, David muttered, "None."

"What's that? I'm sorry, I didn't hear you! Did you say, 'NONE!?'"

Safia let out a little chuckle as she saw the two boys sitting down on the bench and opening their sports drinks. Kenji happened to look over at her and saw her. Their eyes met for a moment, and Kenji, in full testosterone-driven glee, gave her a double bicep pose as he yelled, "Did you see these guns humiliate my child here? He's my son, now. I own him. You need yard work done? I'll send my little kid here over to do it for you." David nudged Kenji in the ribs, and they went back to their teenage-boy exchange with each other.

David asked, "Double bicep pose? Really? Bruh! What's with that?"

"I don't know, man. It just happened."

"Real smooth," David giggled.

On the other end of the floor, Safia was amused and confused. "What is with Kenji today?"

"I don't know," Sam replied. "But the last time I saw a boy do that, he was flirting... trying to show off, you know? You don't think he's interested in you like that, do you?"

"Kenji?" Safia exclaimed in the same overgrown whisper that had become the norm of the day. "Ewww! That's disgusting. Why would you say something like that?"

"You asked a question. I gave you my best answer. Look. I'm just sayin' that that kind of stupid usually comes from boys who are trying to impress girls they like. That's all. I really have no idea what is with him today."

"Well... don't ever say anything like that again. Kenji and I have known each other our whole lives. We were raised together. He's like... a brother... or maybe at least a cousin or something, you know? So... that... what you said... gross. That would be totally weird."

Stunned by Safia's response, Sam said, "Well. Like I said: you asked me what I thought that stupid stuff means... and I told you what it usually means. Whether that's what it means or not, I don't know. All I know is you gotta pick up your game. If that's the best you can do against gym class girls, what you gonna do in a real game when the coach subs you in and you're up against real competition? We're in trouble."

"I know. It's just... Angie. I still feel really bad about that."

"Well... you gotta get over that sooner or later." Pausing all her movements to stare Safia down, she added, "I prefer sooner."

The girls' basketball coach came over and called for the team. "Okay, listen up. All y'all listen up. All you young ladies, team, no team, doesn't matter. In basketball, in sports... in life... sometimes your teammate can't go. Something has happened, something is wrong, they're off their game, they're injured... and it's next man up... or woman in this case... you've gotta cover each other's weakness by lending your strengths to each other. For instance, Safia had a poor shooting day today. Her hands probably still hurt from the incident this weekend. Now, she's normally a hot shooter off the bench and I have no doubt that she'll be ready come game time. But she had a poor shooting day today. What should she have done? She should have relied more on her passing skills to get the ball into the hands of someone who was having a better day shooting. Instead, Tamika kept feeding her the ball when she couldn't get dribble penetration late in the possession and that didn't leave Safia with time to pass, only shoot.

Tamika should have passed the ball to Safia earlier in the possession and let her distribute the ball around and back to her when she made her cut so she could get penetration to the basket and get the easy lay-up. Or, she could have rotated around and got the pass at the top of the arc and taken the three herself. When you see your teammate is in trouble... and this is a life lesson, too, not just basketball... when you see someone is in trouble and you have the ability to cover their weaknesses, you have to step in and change things up, cover their weaknesses with your strengths. Otherwise, when someone is down, they'll keep fallin' down... and we're only as strong as the weakest of us. You understand? We're only as strong as the weakest of us. So lend your strength to one another. Okay? Don't let basketball season roll around and we have to address this again. Fix it now, ladies. Okay? Everyone get cleaned up and get on to your next class."

As her female classmates headed to the locker room, Safia looked again at Angie and her injured hands. The coach's words reverberated within her, and her heart was broken for Angie. She began to wonder if there was something she could do to make things right. Safia decided to be brave and push through the awkwardness. She walked over to Angie and said, "Hey."

Angie took a step back in fear as she responded with, "What?" Safia was perplexed by Angie's reaction. "What do you want, Douglas? Look, I'm sorry, okay? I don't want any trouble."

"No. No. It's not like that," Safia reassured.

"Then... what? What do you want?" Angie replied in confusion.

"So... I know you hate math and all and... well... I'm pretty good at math and... I actually like math, if you believe that, so... I was wondering if you... wanted any help with math? Obviously, you can't even write. So, I could write it for you and... if you get stuck, you know, I..."

"No," Angie decided. "I don't want your help."

"But I want to help..."

"I don't need your charity, Douglas. Okay?" Angie fired back, stinging Safia's feelings a little. "Just... leave me alone. Please leave me alone."

Safia watched as Angie abruptly turned and walked quickly away, her two hands help up in front of her to ensure that they didn't bump anyone or anything on the way out. Safia whispered in disappointment and shame, "But... I didn't say 'I'm sorry' yet."

"Did you get the email I sent you, Chief?" Terry Tolliver asked of Daniel Douglas.

"I'm looking at it right now."

"Well, that's the names and pertinent information of the so-called Firefly Bandits. Phillip and my guys are just waiting for the judge to issue a warrant and we'll pick 'em up right away. I wanted to let you know where we're at in the process and to let you know that this will all be over soon enough."

"I really appreciate that, Detective Tolliver," Daniel replied in relief. "This thing… we've had a devil of a time trying to deal with it."

"Well, it's almost over. Uh, tell me, Chief Douglas: do you recognize any of the names on the list? Most of them have priors and it's possible that you've crossed paths with them before?"

Chief Douglas printed out the email as he looked at the names on the screen. As soon as the document finished printing, he reached to his printer and switched his eyes from the screen to the paper which he now held in his hand. "I can't say that I've ever heard of any of them."

"Well, I wasn't sure if the attack on you was just because we were breathing down their necks real hard, or if it was something personal from the past. Our songbird here reassures us that they didn't send that package and that they're just a bunch of two-bit bandits. But their leader has all the knowledge and experience necessary to pull off a stunt like that on his own. So I was hoping one of those names would jump off the page for you."

"No. Nothing here rings a bell."

"Well, we'll know more after we pick 'em up. Until then, just keep your eyes and ears open and we'll let you know when we've got 'em."

"Sure thing. Thanks for all you guys are doing over there. We really appreciate it."

"Hey. They mess with one of you guys, they mess with all of us. Right?" declared Detective Tolliver.

"Absolutely," agreed Chief Douglas. "Absolutely. Thank you so much. Call me when there's more."

"Will do. Bye now."

"Good-bye," Daniel Douglas said as he ended the call. He thought for a moment about his wife and quickly made the call on his cell phone.

When he heard the call connect on the other end, he didn't even give her time to answer. "Hello, Beautiful."

"Hello, Handsome. To what do I owe the pleasure of this call?"

"In my hand I hold the names, addresses, and other pertinent information on every member of the Firefly Bandits."

"Oh, that's wonderful! Oh, thank You, Jesus!"

"Yep. They're waiting for the judge to issue the warrants and they'll have 'em in custody in no time."

"Awesome! I have several friends here at the DA who would love to prosecute. They're practically lining up to get at these guys."

"Well, whoever gets 'em, I think it's gonna be a slam dunk walk in the park kind of thing."

"Me, too. All you have to do is prove they did one job and you've basically proven they did them all. Same M.O., same evidence, same everything. The DA is gonna put them away for a good little while."

"Yeah, I hope so. These guys are nuts. Anyway, I just wanted to call and let you know. Things turned around in a real hurry, didn't they? I mean... it's... it's really kinda weird that we went so quickly from the ER to this moment as I currently hold all their names here in my hand."

As the circle of friends met outside the school building, they finalized their plans for the remainder of the day. David was already off to football practice, more his sport than basketball. Kenji and Sam were headed to the library to work on a computer science project. It was decided that they would meet at the secret room at six-thirty, or whenever David got there from football practice. "So what are you doing now, Saf?" Sam asked. "Do you want to come to the library with us?"

Safia couldn't help but notice a little tension in Kenji's face when Sam made the invitation. She was quite curious, for sure. But she had other plans. "No, thanks. I... have a visit I need to make."

"Who... who are you visiting?" Kenji asked, not jealous, but trying to not sound jealous.

"I'm going to visit Angie."

"Angie Who?" Kenji asked with genuine puzzle.

"She means Angry Angie," Sam answered with a little disapproval in her voice and a little judgment on her face as she studied Safia's eyes.

"Her real name is Angie Dunlifsky. And she's a human being. And I feel like I need to talk to her. And this is hard enough to do without my best friends in the whole wide world giving me grief about it."

Sam lowered her head a bit and said, "Sorry, Saf. I'm... really sorry. I hadn't thought of it that way. Just... be careful. I hear her family isn't the best."

"Yeah," Kenji agreed. "You need to make your visit, say your peace, and get out."

"Then that's what I'll do," agreed Safia. "So... wish me luck."

"Actually, I'll probably pray for you," Sam jested.

"I'll probably need you to," Safia replied with a smile.

"What do you mean they can't get arrest warrants?" Jerrica Douglas demanded of her husband.

"Somebody signed something in the wrong place, and now none of the information the police got from McGuiness can be used to acquire an arrest warrant, or even a search warrant. They have McGuiness on facial recognition, but his lawyer arrived and lawyered up and now it will be weeks before we get any information out of him that we can use to go after the other three. In the meantime, who knows what kind of danger they'll pose?"

"Well, we know who they are and where they are. It's just a matter of time before we come across something admissible that can be used to get a warrant, even if it's just a search warrant. All it takes is a little evidence and we can make an arrest. Once they're behind bars, they'll turn on each other and, before long, we'll have hard evidence to go along with it."

"But... in the meantime... who's to stop them from doing more damage... or maybe even something worse?"

Safia stood in front of the apartment building where Angie lived. She was forcing out a little smile as she whispered, "Sam, I sure hope you're praying for me."

Moments later, Safia was standing in front of the door, knocking a gentle knock, unsure of how aggressively she should be knocking. The door opened, and the stepfather, Doug McKinney, stood in the opening, reeking of alcohol as he lost his balance and decided to lean on the door casing for assistance. "Can I help you?" he belched.

"Uhm, yes, Sir. I'm here to see Angie Dunlifsky. Is this her house?"

"Angie!" an obviously drunken Doug yelled. "You got a little friend here to see you!"

Angie came quickly and sheepishly from the back of the house, trying to hide the bleeding lip and the fresh black eye she was now sporting. She took one look at Safia and softly said, "She's not my friend."

"Well, I don't care who she is. Make it quick! You got chores to do!"

"What is it, Douglas?" Angie asked, half embarrassed and half angry.

"Uh…," was all Safia could manage to get out as she looked at Angie's face and then she looked at Angie's stepfather. This was not the Doug she had met before who seemed to be reasonable, responsible, and together. This was a scary, sick man.

"What are you lookin' at, Douglas? My life?"

"Uhm… I'm… I'm sorry. I just came here to… apologize for what happened to your hands."

Angie was caught completely off guard by the apology. Her countenance toward Safia changed as she said, "Yeah. Well. No big. It was my fault anyway. I hit you."

"Yeah, well… I was hoping that we could… maybe… start over and… not fight anymore and…"

"I have two broken hands. I'm not fighting anyone any time soon. What do you want to do? Holds hands and sing campfire songs? Not doing that any time soon, either."

"No, I was just… I was just hoping that…" Safia was stumped. She took a deep breath and explained, "Look. I feel bad about what happened, and I wanted to apologize. And I was hoping that, while we're at it, we could bury whatever hatchet there may be."

Angie stared at Safia for what seemed a small eternity before answering, "You know what, Douglas? Apology accepted. Like I said: it's my fault anyway. But I have no desire to be buddies. Okay?"

Safia nodded, glad to have forgiveness. That's what she really came here for anyway. "That's enough for me. Thanks. I'll… see you at school or something."

Angie was still confounded by Safia's kindness. "Uh, yeah."

"Bye," Safia said to end the awkwardness.

"Bye," Angie mocked back before closing the door slowly on Safia's face.

Safia stood there frozen, amazed, and perplexed at what had just happened. She finally turned to walk away. As she did, she heard Doug's voice thundering, "That's the girl you hurt yourself hitting? That little pipsqueak? Huh?"

Safia froze again, and her shoulders shuttered when she heard the crashing of furniture and decorations from inside the apartment. She heard Doug stomping and pounding as he yelled at Angie to take out the garbage. "But I can't!" Angie cried out in tears. "My hands!"

"Oh, your hands, huh?" Doug yelled. "Well, if you can't do your chores because of your hands, I'm gonna have to teach you how to not fight! And if you DO fight, WIN, you stupid MORON!" Safia heard the blows and the screams from Angie. She hated feeling powerless to stop abuse like this.

Then, she heard the coach's words echoing through her head about how people need to lend their strength to others when they are weak or in trouble. The reluctant hero didn't even have time to think before she was pounding on the door. "Mr. McKinney, open the door!"

"Go away, little brat!" Doug yelled. "We don't want none!"

Safia knocked again, rattling the hinges almost loose from the door frame. "Open this door… now!"

Doug turned toward the door and yelled, "Who are you to talk to me like that, you little toothpick? Mind your own business!"

Safia met the limits of her patience, and her fear for Angie's safety overrode any apprehension she once had. Suddenly the door of the apartment burst open. Safia entered to find Doug standing over Angie's cowered form as he held a broken broom handle in his hand. "You wanna hit somebody so bad? Why don't you try that on me?"

"If you insist!" Doug declared before swinging the broom handle at Safia. She raised her forearm up to block it, and the wooden handle broke across the strength of her radius bone. She winced in pain only a little. Doug looked at the remnant of the broken broom handle in his hand. "Okay. I know how to fix this!" he said as he drew back his fist.

"I really wouldn't if I were you," Safia warned.

Doug threw his best right-handed roundhouse punch to the left side of Safia's face. He screamed over and over as if he had fallen into a fire when his hand shattered against Safia's cheek bone. Doug fell to the floor, holding his right hand in his left as he was overcome with the immense pain of the injury. He managed to look up at Safia and questioned, "What are you?"

Safia looked down at this pathetic excuse for a man and replied, "I'm just a girl... a girl who will be back if you ever lay a hand on my friend here again. And next time, I'll be throwing the punches. You understand?" Shaking from the pain of the injury and quivering in fear, Doug nodded his head to indicate that he understood. Safia reached her hand for Angie's arm and helped her to her feet. "Come on. Let's go for a walk. Your stepfather needs some time alone to re-think his life."

As soon as the two girls were in the stairwell headed to the bottom floor, Safia apologized, "I'm sorry I butted in. I just couldn't hear that and do nothing."

"No. No. Don't apologize. I've been wanting to do something like that to Doug for years."

"You mean this has been happening for years?" Safia asked in wonder.

"Yeah. Seven years, I think. He was kinda cool for the first two years after he married my mom. Then he started drinking, and it was all downhill from there real fast. At first it was just too many smacks with the belt when he whipped me. But then he started getting worse and worse, he started hitting my mom, too, and... well... you know the rest. It's been like this for about seven years. By the way... the gash on your arm is already healed up. That's pretty cool actually."

Safia now realized that, in her haste to stop the abuse, she had dropped the charade and fully let Angie in on her secret. "Uh, thanks. So... seven years of that crap? Wow. No wonder you're always angry." Safia thought and a curious wrinkle appeared on her forehead as she asked, "So you weren't always angry and mean?"

"You mean a bully? No, I always hated bullies when I was little. But when you live with a bully, eventually it becomes all you know. But I don't think I have to be a bully anymore... thanks to you."

"No thanks necessary."

"No. I mean it." Angie stopped walking and turned to Safia, who took the cue and stopped walking as well. "Thanks, Douglas. You really helped me out today. Whatever this is that's going on with you... your secret is safe with me."

"Oh," Safia exhaled, letting out the tension. "You have no idea how relieved I am to hear that from you. If I could only hear that from Jimmy Willis... my stress level would plummet."

"Oh, yeah. Jimmy," Angie said. "Hey, don't worry about Jimmy. He's my cousin and he knows about Doug. He knows about the fight at school, too. He won't shut up about it... but just to me. I'll have a talk with him and, if you don't mind me telling him what happened here today, I'm pretty sure that Jimmy won't say a word to anybody. He hates Doug almost as much as I do, so... you probably just made a fan out of Jimmy Willis."

"That's probably the best thing I've heard all day," Safia responded.

"Yeah, well... I guess if you... really want to hold hands and sing campfire songs..." Angie said in jest, showing a completely new side to her personality, "I'm game, but...you'll have to wait a while for the holding hands part, right?"

"Yeah." The two girls giggled a little together. Then, Safia asked, "So what are you gonna do about Doug and his injuries?"

"Well," began Angie, "I'm probably gonna have to walk him to the ER, and then he's gonna have to tell the ER doctor that this time HE punched a wall." Safia smiled as Angie continued, "Irony: gotta love it."

"Yeah. Irony... sure is something else. So... that's it, then. We're friends now, right?"

"Whoa, Douglas. Whoa. I don't think you're cool enough to be seen with me in public." Safia was trying not to show her disappointment. And she was surprised that she was truly a little disappointed. "Just kidding," Angie said with a smile. "But... you know what you said about math earlier?"

"Yeah?" Safia responded.

"It's true. I'm not gonna be able to do my math homework with two bum hands. So... can you come by Tuesdays? Right after school?"

"Uhm... yeah. I can. But are you sure you want to do this?"

"Are you kidding? I'd want to do it just to see Doug's reaction when he goes to the door and it's you standin' there." The two girls shared one more laugh before Angie said, "Well, I gotta get home. I need to be there when my mom gets home so I can control the narrative. It shouldn't be too hard considering how drunk he is. So… thanks, Douglas. You're my hero… and my tutor."

"No prob," Safia answered back. "You need help with the door?"

"Uhm… I think you permanently opened the door, so… no." The two girls shared one last smile before Angie started back up the stairs.

Just as Angie disappeared up the steps, Safia's phone rang. She swiped right and put the phone to her ear. "Hi, Mom. What's up?" A huge smile came across her face as she said, "That's great!" Then, the smile disappeared. "Why not?!" she exclaimed. "But that makes no sense! Their names and addresses and information are all on Dad's desk, but no one can do anything about it? That's not right!" As she listened to her mother explain the situation, the expression on Safia's face slowly morphed into one of determination.

Safia sat in front of her circle of friends in the secret meeting place as she concluded, "So that's when I decided that someone CAN do something about it. I've got these special powers. And I CAN do good with them. What happened at Angie's apartment building proves it."

"Saf, I already told you," Sam responded. "These powers belong to you. You can do whatever YOU want to with them. So if you want to do the superhero thing, count me in. I'll do whatever I can to help you."

"Yeah, me, too," agreed Kenji. "We're on your side all the way."

"Don't look at me," David said with a huge smile. "I've been on board with the superhero thing from the get go. You know I'm in."

"Good," Safia said. "So I want you guys to help me learn how to control my powers. Because I'm going to catch the Firefly Bandits. And you guys are gonna help me do it."

————— ⟨⟩ —————

CHAPTER FIVE

THE HERO EMERGES

[Kilwa region of East Africa, 1752]

Sirclantis stood guard outside the regeneration chamber, hoping that the technology would work on this human just as it did on him. But he couldn't be too sure. No one of his kind had ever tried to use this technology on an alien before. But if there was even a chance that it would work, Sirclantis was willing to take that chance, regardless of the consequences. He wasn't supposed to share his technology with alien races, especially with one so primitive. He wasn't even supposed to be on Earth. And he wasn't supposed to be seen or detected by any alien races on any of the planets he visited. And yet, he couldn't help but try to save the life of this Earth creature who had sacrificed its life for him.

The regeneration cycle was taking much longer than usual. There were sounds and lights that Sirclantis had never seen before as the computer searched for answers to restore the physiology of this alien it had never encountered before. Sirclantis waited for what seemed like an eternity, hoping that this would work. Suddenly, he heard a noise in the distance as the first signs of light began to turn the black sky to the deepest blue he had ever seen. He took a few steps out toward the noise and peered into the early dawn. He was now able to recognize the sounds as the rhythmic patterns of primitive percussion instruments. It didn't take Sirclantis long to realize that these were the drums of war. Through the early dawn light amid the backdrop of what was now a blue-gray sky came the silhouettes of warriors. As the ranks of the warriors made their way from the horizon down into the valley, Sirclantis was able to see their numbers, about fifty. Fifty Adui warriors were indeed an intimidating sight, even to someone as strong and skilled as Sirclantis. The Adui had indeed returned with the numbers necessary to overcome him.

He gripped his two-bladed weapon tightly in his grasp, and then he began to swing it loosely in his fingers as if warming up for battle. Soon enough the platoon of Adui warriors was lined up before him only sixty feet away. Their general came to the front of the ranks to look the giant in his face. He stared at him fearlessly for several moments. Then, he looked down at the bodies of the slain Adui who had attacked earlier, General Kamili and his subordinates.

The drums were finally silenced as the general held up his hand. "I am General Mosi of the Adui. I have come that you might answer for your crimes against my people. What have you to say for yourself?"

The device on Sirclantis's chest translated the general's charge. It also translated as Sirclantis gave his response, "If these lands belong to you, then I have trespassed and will leave as soon as I am able. But if these lands are in dispute, then I will stay as long as I like." The Adui warriors grumbled in disapproval, but their general held up his hand again for silence.

"The land is indeed in dispute!" declared General Mosi. "You have committed no crime of trespass. But what have you to say about these slain Adui who lay before you?"

Sirclantis stood tall and proud as he boldly answered, "These men attacked the man who saved my life. I stopped them from killing him in order to pay my debt. But then, they attacked me. I merely defended myself."

"But surely one as great and powerful as you could have defended himself without killing them. So why, then, do the bodies of my brothers lay in the sand at your feet?"

Sirclantis growled as he prepared his final answer. "I judged them worthy of death, and so rewarded them."

The Adui warriors grumbled even louder this time. General Mosi held up his hand once again for silence. He gazed upon this large creature for several moments before releasing a smile. "Then I will show you the same courtesy. I judge you worthy of death, and we will so reward you." The smile was quickly replaced by a scowl of anger as the general struck the butt of his spear on the ground. On cue, the ranks of the Adui warriors quickly spread in either direction by rows until they made a circle which surrounded Sirclantis and his ship. "When the sun rises today, we will give your carcass as a sacrifice of peace to the beasts of the earth." The general gave a signal, and the circle of warriors took a giant step forward as they pointed their spears inward toward Sirclantis. The general gave another signal, and the circle grew yet smaller. Sirclantis growled as he prepared for the ensuing battle. But his attackers had the numbers to their advantage. There was a very good chance that he would not survive.

Suddenly, there came a sound from the regeneration chamber, and everyone looked on as the lid moved to the open position, and Bakari emerged, complete and whole. Sirclantis was overwhelmed with joy that it had worked. Bakari quickly jumped from the enormous pod and came to his friend's side.

General Mosi turned to one of the soldiers and demanded, "I thought you said he was dead."

"He was, General. I saw him die with my own eyes. I saw the giant lay his lifeless body on that thing and mourn."

Sirclantis growled and the device translated, "You need to run. I can handle this."

"I doubt that greatly, my friend. Besides… you saved my life. Now, we fight together."

"I didn't save it for you to lose it before the Sun rises. When I engage them, you need to find a hole in the circle and run."

"Well, I'm not doing that, so you'd better get ready to fight together. How many of them can you take?"

Sirclantis gave in to Bakari's demands and replied, "Not many… perhaps thirty-five."

"That's not many?" Bakari asked with amazement.

"Not when there are fifty," Sirclantis answered with clarity.

"So… what's the battle plan?" Bakari asked.

At that moment, General Mosi gave the order and the Adui attacked. Sirclantis answered Bakari's question by quickly saying, "Fight!"

Sirclantis tried to take on as many Adui as he could to keep Bakari from being so easily outnumbered, but the attack was fierce. At times, Bakari would fight one-on-one while Sirclantis took on seven at a time. But at other times, Bakari would find himself outnumbered, and Sirclantis would find a way to work over to Bakari and engage his attackers. Several Adui warriors were now slain at the hands of Sirclantis, but there were still more than forty who were learning his fighting style and adjusting. And the pace was beginning to wear on the giant. He feared that he would soon have to abandon Bakari to fend for himself or see them both die.

Just as Sirclantis was about to lose hope, a line of Adui warriors made their charge at him, but the body of an Adui warrior suddenly came flying through the air and knocked the attackers off their feet. Sirclantis turned to see Bakari fiercely fighting, quickly and easily overpowering his attackers with brute strength. One Adui warrior, whose spear had been broken, swung the butt end of it like a club against Bakari's head. Sirclantis watched with amazement as the wooden handle shattered into splinters against Bakari's head, having no effect on Bakari but to anger him all the more as he reached over and raised the Adui in the air with one hand and threw him some eighty feet away. Somehow, Bakari was now as strong and powerful as Sirclantis, perhaps even more. Turning his attention to those Adui nearest him, Sirclantis now went on the attack, and the two quickly turned the tide, discomfiting the platoon of Adui warriors who once thought victory was assured.

The dust began to settle as the Sun peaked over the horizon. There stood Bakari and Sirclantis side-by-side in the middle of the battle site, surrounded by the bodies of slain Adui. One lone Adui was still standing, the scout who had gone back and retrieved General Mosi and the platoon of warriors. Bakari shouted at him, "Go back to the Adui! Go! And tell your King Sefu what you have seen here!" As Bakari was speaking, Sirclantis was amazed to see Bakari's wounds rapidly healing right before his eyes. The scout also saw this and began to tremble with fear. Bakari continued, "Tell him to send no more Adui to this place, or they will suffer the same fate! Go!"

As the Adui scout ran back to his people, Sirclantis said, "The regeneration device has had an unexpected effect on you, my friend. You now possess the power of many. But I must know. What will you do with this power?"

"I don't know. It feels... so strange... to be this strong. And my wounds... they are gone."

"Yes. Healed before my eyes as I watched," Sirclantis stated. "I have never seen anything like that. And from what I saw when you fought the three before, this is not normal for your kind."

"No. It is not normal."

"Then, again, I ask: what will you do with this power? You have a decisive advantage over anyone you face. Will you wield this power responsibly to protect the weak, or will you use it for war and conquest?"

"If I were a man of war and conquest, I would not have saved your life," Bakari answered bluntly. "And if you believed me to be a man of war and conquest, you would not have saved mine."

"Then you must swear to me to only use this power to protect the weak and to defend what is right and noble... or I will have to kill you myself before I leave this planet."

Bakari was blown away by the words of Sirclantis. "Kill me?"

"Yes!" confirmed Sirclantis. "It would be irresponsible of me to give this power to you and then leave your planet without knowing that it is safe from you. Therefore swear to me that you will protect the weak, preserve the peace whenever possible, that you will stand for justice, and that you will defend liberty. Swear this on your own soul."

Bakari nodded his head in full understanding as he said, "I swear to you that I will only do with this power what is right and true, that I will not be selfish with it, and that I will only harm those who seek to harm others."

Sirclantis replied, "Then use your new strength to help me pick up my ship. I need to get to the underside to make repairs. I am on an important mission, and I must leave soon."

[Modern-Day Atlanta, Georgia, U.S.A.] Wednesday morning came, and the circle of friends found themselves huddled together outside Tweed-Johnson High School reviewing the plan for what would happen after school. "Okay, so the tech is up and running," celebrated Sam. "I can see everything you can see, hear everything you can hear, and you can hear me. It looks just like a regular pair of glasses. Works the same way your mask does. If you want to give it a try today, just give me the signal and we're a go."

"I'll be your eyes and ears in the field," Kenji said.

"Why you?" asked David.

"Let's see. You'll be late because of football practice, and I have martial arts training."

"Fair point," David agreed.

"And with Angie and Jimmy no longer an issue, there's no reason why we can't pull this off and keep my identity a secret," Safia assured. "So, after school today, I'll drop by the fire station to get my dad to sign something or okay something and, while I'm there, I'll find the list and take a look at it…"

"And I'll take a picture of it through the cam…" Sam interjected.

"And then we'll pay the Firefly Bandits a little visit. All we need is enough evidence to provide reasonable suspicion. If we drop it off anonymously to the police station and they get it, they can get a warrant and go find everything else."

"And if one of them comes home while you're at his house?" David asked.

"I think I can handle myself," Safia reassured.

"With one evening of training?" Kenji asked.

"Yeah, but I really don't have to be that good at fighting when I'm super strong and my bones apparently don't break anymore."

"Yeah, but what if you get gashed open and lose a lot of blood?" David asked.

"And what if one of them pulls out a gun?" Kenji added.

"That's not gonna happen. I'm gonna sneak in, grab some evidence, and sneak out. No problem," Safia reassured again.

"And what are you looking for?" Sam asked.

"You'll know it when I see it, right?" Safia asked with a smile.

"Uh, yeah. Absolutely," Sam agreed.

"Okay, then. Let's do it!" Safia declared. "This morning, school. This afternoon, the Firefly Bandits. Tomorrow?"

"Pizza?" David suggested.

Everyone exploded with smiles as Safia decided, "Tomorrow, pizza. Okay, you guys. Let's go."

Zuri Walker examined closely the contents of the envelope that Jacob Tyler Mathew had retrieved for her from her contact inside public records. "What are you looking for?" Jacob Tyle Mathew asked. "A lost relative or something?"

"I already told you: I'm looking for a hero."

"Yeah, but what are you looking for in all that garbage?"

"Mr. Mathew, I'm not looking through garbage. I'm looking through public records. This is history and I, for one, greatly appreciate history. As a historian, I have had the privilege of witnessing the rise and fall of great civilizations, kingdoms, nations, groups, and... families. I am looking through the public records trying to piece together the history of the Douglas family. I want to know how they came to live in Atlanta, from whence did they come, when did the move here, who was with them at the time, etcetera, etcetera, etcetera. Putting together an accurate timeline of events could give me the understanding I need to act with more precision instead of taking stabs in the murky water."

"Murky water?" Mathew puzzled aloud.

"It's a reference to a primal form of fishing that is still in use in more of the world than you would believe, Mr. Mathew. Really... you need some culture. Now, if you don't mind, I have serious work to do. Why don't you read a thesaurus or something?"

"What's a thesiosaurus?"

Irritated with the ignorance and lack of intelligence exhibited by Mathew, Ms. Walker responded, "Well, I would guess it's a make-believe dinosaur made up by someone who doesn't know what a thesaurus is, but if you go read a thesaurus, maybe you'll learn more about it. Go. Shoo. I have a lot to do. And my alter ego, Ms. Bridgewater, has an appointment to keep today."

Mathew grumbled, "I know what a thesaurus is. I just didn't hear you."

Safia walked down the hallway of Tweed-Johnson High School on a high feeling that originated from the thought that all was right with the world. She was feeling pretty indestructible as her day went on. A smile from Angie Dunlifsky, a nod and a smile from Angie's cousin, Jimmy Willis, and Safia was assured that all was well.

She got her test back in Mrs. Gramble's class and beheld the score: ninety-six percent. With grammar being her weakest subject, a high A was like Christmas to her. By third period Spanish class, Safia had gained such momentum that nothing could stop her. She looked over at Sam, who was wearing a headset as she studied Mandarin Chinese and Swahili instead of Spanish. Sam was already fluent in Spanish, both the traditional, proper version spoken in Spain and the Mexican version popular in the Americas. She was instead using this opportunity to study Chinese because of its importance in the world and Swahili because of its importance to her best friend's family. They gave each other nods of approval and encouragement as they plowed through the language class with ease.

Lunch was baked chicken, turnip greens, sweet potato soufflé, mixed fruit, and a dinner roll. Safia thought to herself that, if the chicken were only fried, this meal could almost pass as soul food. She added a little seasoning to it and enjoyed it immensely.

During fifth period, Ms. Sawyer came to Safia's desk. "I couldn't help but notice you're kinda flyin' through this stuff. Perhaps you'd like to borrow this book?" she posed as she presented to her a book on introduction to trigonometry with real-life applications. Safia's smile spanned her whole face as she took the book in hand. Ms. Sawyer added, "These applications make the world of math come alive, and I think you'll enjoy getting a head-start on things."

"Thank you so much," Safia said as she took the book and hugged it with pride and self-confidence swelling inside her.

"Just remember to return it when you're done," Ms. Sawyer said with a smile. "That book is from my private library." Safia's pride and self-confidence swelled even more as she opened the book and turned to the first page with anticipation.

At gym, Safia was full of energy and life. Tamika was passing the ball earlier in each possession, and Safia was able to distribute the ball to her teammates. The offense for her team started producing at a high level, and Safia found numerous opportunities to take outside shots, including several three-pointers. She ended the game with eighteen points, eleven assists, and two steals. At the end of class, the girls' basketball coach came over and patted her on the head. "Great game, Douglas. Keep that up and I'll have to give you more playing time. You, too, Tamika. Way to involve everyone ladies. I want to see that come basketball season." Praise from the coach is one of the greatest rewards for any athlete, and Safia was now riding higher than ever. This would quite possibly be the best day of her life.

Seventh period finally came, and the tenth graders were summoned to the assembly to meet the representative from FTDVA. Safia and her friends quickly found a table in the conference room where they could sit together to hear the spiel from the representative, who walked to the podium and tested the microphone. She tapped it to produce a thumping noise and then leaned in and said, "Testing, one, two. Can you guys all hear me?" The students nodded, a few responded verbally, and Zuri Walker introduced herself. "Good afternoon, students. My name is Tiffany Bridgewater, and I represent the Foundation for Teen Development in Vital Aptitudes. Our non-profit organization seeks out young people with potential to help us advance the sciences at an expedited rate and then supports their learning with career path advising, scholarships, grants, and advanced entry into certain schools of study. We have reviewed your standardized test results, as well as certain academic records, and the review has indicated that there may be several students at Tweed-Johnson High School who could benefit from the assistance which our organization provides. Also, we feel like the world could benefit from what those students have to offer, and we have, therefore, chosen Tweed-Johnson as our state of Georgia school of focus. What we're going to do today is have you guys move around to the different stations we have set up at the back of the room, and we want you to see the many different opportunities that lay before you in S.T.E.M. studies at the next level of education, in the work force, in the government, in the military, in research, and beyond. Also, there is a list by the main entrance with the names of fifteen students that we have identified as having tremendous promise based upon your academic history, standardized testing scores, and teacher recommendations. This does not mean that the other students may not qualify for any of our programs, so feel free to look around and come see me at the table, but I want at least the names on that list to come see me at the table so I can tell you what we have to offer. Also, as a show of appreciation for the hard work you have all put into your education, I am pleased to announce that the

FTDVA is donating three thousand dollars toward the purchase of a set of new, state-of-the-art computers for your science department." The assembly buzzed with excitement and approval. "These computers will be available to all students at Tweed-Johnson to further your education and hopefully nurture your interest in the sciences. Thank you and congratulations to each and every one of you on achieving at a very high level as a class. It is rare that we find an entire grade that works so hard on their studies, and I commend you. Now, please visit the centers in the back, and I look forward to speaking to each of you in person at my table in the corner over here. Thank you."

The students worked the room, carefully and gleefully studying each display that this Ms. Bridgewater had set up. Most of the students were truly intrigued by the many opportunities represented. A few were just glad to be out of class and pretended to be interested as they cut jokes together. Safia and her friends were quick to go to the list, hoping their names would be there. Sure enough, all four of their names were on the list. "Wow guys," David said. "There are only fifteen names on this list, and we're all on it. What do you think of that, huh?"

"I think it means we're the nerds of the bunch, David," Sam responded.

"Yeah, we're all geniuses, right?" David added.

"Not all of us," Kenji said. "Just you two guys… unless Safia has been holding out."

"Nope," Safia responded immediately. "136."

Sam responded, "Whoa, Saf! That's extremely high."

"Really?" Safia came back with surprise. "I mean, I know it's high, but it's not THAT high. Is it?"

"Is that the Stanford-Binet test?" Sam asked.

"I don't know. I took it here in school in third grade."

"That's the Stanford-Binet," Sam concluded. "That means that you are in the gifted range, which is higher than superior intelligence. Consider this: only five percent score above 125, so, yeah… you're a nerd, just like us." Safia smiled a little as Sam turned to Kenji. "How about you, Kenji? I know you've got be a genius."

"Nope. 126 on the Stanford-Binet. Not even gifted. I'm officially the dumbest person in our circle of friends."

"Then how do you make straight A's?" David begged.

"I do this ancient Japanese art form called studying. It works really well. All I do is study until I know and understand everything, no matter how long it takes. So it doesn't matter what my IQ is, because my work ethic more than makes up for any cognitive deficiencies I may have."

"Cognitive deficiencies?" Sam said with a smirk of sarcasm. "You're still in the upper range of superior intelligence."

"Yeah, well… both my parents are geniuses, so I'm a regular disappointment. My brother has an IQ of like 144 or something. I have no idea what happened to me. Maybe I was sick or something on test day. I don't know. And I try not to think about it. Because, like I said, my work ethic more than makes up for any deficiencies I may or may not have. Like my grandfather says: disciplined effort is the greatest advantage one can possess."

"Well, I'm going to go over and talk to the lady," said Sam. "I want to know what kind of scholarships and grants I can get. That stuff would be such a life saver for my college career."

"I'm going with her," Safia agreed.

"We'll be along in a sec," David said. "I want to check out this computer science display and get my tech on."

"Computer science?" Sam asked with intrigue.

"Uhm, yeah. I've—I've always… been interested in computer science. I just never put my mind to it because I was busy with other things. But I'm thinking about clearing out some space on my agenda to get all tech-y."

Sam smiled and commented as she and Safia walked away, "I'm not sure 'tech-y' is a word, but… let me know if there's anything you think I should check out."

"Okay… I will!" David called after her.

Kenji smiled at David, amused at how his gaze lingered on Sam as she and Safia walked over to the table to speak to the representative. "Dude… you got it bad, man. You need to tell her."

"Not yet. Not yet. But… soon. Real soon."

"Yeah?" Kenji pressed.

"Yeah," assured David. "No cap."

"Okay. We'll see."

Safia and Sam waited their turn to see Ms. Bridgewater. Only a few moments passed before it was their turn. Zuri Walker, as Ms. Bridgewater, said, "Hello! Can I have your names?" She lifted a clipboard in her hand as she scanned the names with the pen in her hand.

"Samantha Castillo!" Sam blurted out with excitement.

"Okay, Samantha Castillo Cruz," she said with a perfect accent, "gotcha right here. And you are?" she said glancing up at Safia.

"Safia Douglas."

"Safia Kamaria Douglas," she responded, again in perfect accent, "I gotcha."

"Wow!" Safia said, impressed. "Most people can't pronounce my name just right."

"Mine neither," agreed Sam.

"Well, I've learned to appreciate other languages and cultures. I'm somewhat of a historian, like Ms. Douglas. Your history teacher, Mrs. Thompson, says you make straight A's in history. And languages are beautiful, don't you think so, Ms. Castillo? I hear you're studying Mandarin Chinese and... Swahili? Curious choices. Why did you choose those languages if you don't mind me asking?"

"Well, I'm already fluent in Mexican Spanish as well as traditional Spanish from Spain, so there was no point in me taking the Spanish sequence. So they let me do online learning in other languages of my choice and, well... Mandarin is the most-spoken language in the world, so that was a no-brainer. And Safia's grandfather speaks Swahili, and her names are Swahili, so... I thought it would be fascinating to learn Swahili, especially the names. It's a really beautiful language."

"Yes, it really is," Ms. Bridgewater agreed. "Safia, your grandfather speaks Swahili?"

"Yes, Ma'am. He collects old comics, and some of them have a lot of Swahili in them."

"You're talking about the oldest of the Commander A-Power comics?" Ms. Bridgewater asked.

"Yes, Ma'am," Safia replied.

"Interesting. And I hear that you're quite gifted in mathematics?"

"Uh, yes, Ma'am. But I'm just starting to realize that."

"No, I don't think so," Ms. Bridgewater replied, surprising Safia and Sam. She continued, "I think you've known you were special for some time now. I suspect that you're just starting to accept that."

Safia was nervous and didn't quite understand the answer. But ever the polite southern girl, she said, "Yes, Ma'am. Thank you."

"Now," Ms. Bridgewater continued as she turned to Sam, "you speak Spanish, and you're studying Mandarin Chinese and Swahili. But I understand you speak a good bit of a few different languages. Isn't that right, Ms. Castillo?"

"Uh, yes, Ma'am," Sam answered. "I guess so."

Ms. Bridgewater made direct eye contact as she proceeded. "So, Ms. Castillo." She then asked Sam in perfect Mandarin Chinese, "Nǐ hǎo ma?" *(How are you?)*

Sam responded, "Wǒ hěn hǎo, xiè xiè. Nǐ ne?" *(I'm very good, thank you. And you?)*

"Wǒ hěn hǎo, xiè xiè. Nǐ huì shuō déyǔ ma?" *(I am very good, thank you. Do you also speak German?)*

Sam replied in perfect German, "Ja ich spreche Deutsch." *(Yes, I speak German.)*

"Was ich das problem mit Deutshcen computer?" *(What is the problem with German computers?)*

"An ihrer hardware ist nichts auszusetzen. Sie haben ein problem mit software weil computer programmiert sind in Englisch." *(The basic hardware is written in auszusetzen. They have a problem with the software because the computer programs are written in English.)*

"Sprechen sie Russisch?" *(Do you speak Russian?)*

Sam answered in perfect Russian, "Konechno. Chto by vy khoteli uznat?" *(Of course. What do you want to know?)*

"My, my, my," Zuri Walker replied with amazement. "Aren't you a regular little polyglot?"

"I try. I read a lot of books written in foreign languages about technological and engineering advances. It's the only way to stay ahead of the curve when it comes to computer science applications in the real world. I intend to use my tech skills to make a global impact one day."

Laughing out loud, Ms. Bridgewater declared, "And I have no doubt at all that you will. Wow." She thought for just a moment before asking in perfect Greek, "Xereis na milas elinika?" *(Do you speak Greek?)*

"I'm... sorry?" Sam responded.

"No Greek, huh?" Zuri Walker replied. "Well… someone as young as you needs future goals, right?"

"Uh… yes, Ma'am," Sam said, stunned that she had more than met her match.

"Alright, you smart ladies. We can work on your behalf to get you in line for scholarships and grants for special student projects, but we're going to need your parents' permission to access your academic records and send them to our constituents. So have your parents fill out and sign these forms, and we'll do the rest." She handed them forms and ink pens as she stood to depart them, and then patted them on the shoulder. "Oh, I almost forgot. I have these pendants that I'm supposed to be giving out today and I haven't given out a single one." She turned and retrieved two of them from a bag underneath the table and then put on a big smile as she said, "May I put them on you?"

"Sure," said Sam with excitement.

"Okay, Ms. Castillo," Ms. Bridgewater said with professional courtesy and tenderness. "You first, then." She pinned the little button on her shirt.

Sam looked down at the button and read it aloud, "I am the future of this world. FTDVA."

"You're next, Ms. Douglas," Ms. Bridgewater said.

As Zuri Walker reached to pin the button on Safia's shirt, Sam spoke into her cell phone, "Set reminder." After she heard a beep, she said, "Start Greek classes ASAP."

"OW!" Safia exclaimed.

"Oh, my!" Ms. Bridgewater said. "I am so, so sorry, honey!" Ms. Bridgewater had pricked Safia with the point of the pin on the button, and Safia began to bleed on her shirt. "Oh, dear. Here!" Ms. Bridgewater said as she began to wipe the blood with her handkerchief. "I am so sorry. I cannot believe I just did that. I am so, so sorry."

"It's no big deal," Safia reassured. "Really. It's just a little blood. Look. It's already stopped bleeding."

"Hold on just a second," Ms. Bridgewater said as she remembered. "I think I have some peroxide in my purse." She rifled through her purse with haste and found the peroxide. "Here. I always keep this in case I get a nosebleed. It's a miracle tool getting blood out of clothes if you get it right away." She wadded the handkerchief up and slipped it into her pocket as she doused Safia's shirt with the peroxide and started rubbing the fabric against itself until the blood was gone. "There. I don't see anything. But again, I am so sorry. Are you sure you're okay?"

"Really, it's no big deal," Safia reassured. "It doesn't even hurt anymore. I'm fine."

"Are you sure?" Ms. Bridgewater asked apologetically.

"I'm positive. I feel fine."

"Well... maybe you should pin this on yourself, then," Ms. Bridgewater encouraged.

"Yeah," Safia answered with a smile. "That might be a good idea."

The two giggled off the tension as Ms. Bridgewater said, "Don't forget to get those forms signed by your parents and return them to the office. Okay?"

"Okay. Thanks," Safia replied.

"Yeah. Thanks so much," Sam added. As the two girls walked away, Sam asked, "Are you okay, Saf?"

"Super healing," Safia whispered back. "It's already gone."

"Wow," Sam whispered. "Ms. Bridgewater is amazing, don't you think?"

"Yeah, she's smart. And fluent in more languages than you are I think."

"Maybe. Hey, maybe that'll be me in five to ten more years." Sam puzzled for a moment and asked, "Hey, Saf. What do you think? How old is Ms. Bridgewater?"

"She can't be more than thirty. If I had to guess, I'd say twenty-six. She looks perfect."

"Yeah. Maybe that'll be me when I'm twenty-six: perfect-looking genius polyglot."

As the girls walked farther away from her, Zuri Walker pulled the handkerchief out of her pocket and looked at the blood she had collected with a smile of accomplishment and wonder, anxious now for the rouse to end so she could get to her real work.

After school, the circle of friends met outside the back entrance as David prepared for football practice. Safia held up the permission form from Ms. Bridgewater and said, "I have my reason to go by the fire station and see my dad. I'm gonna let him know about all the opportunities and get him to sign this form. While he's signing the form, I'll be wearing these new sunglasses that Sam gave me. All I have to do is look at the list and Sam will take a picture of it."

"We'll be recording all the time," Sam added, "but I will need to get a snapshot to make sure it's readable. Otherwise, it should be a piece of cake."

"And then we'll set up operational headquarters in the secret room," Kenji added, "and launch the mission from there."

"And I'll be at football practice and miss the whole thing!" David said with disappointment.

"Yeah, but we'll be waiting for you at the secret room. So as soon as practice is over, meet us there and we'll go through our findings together."

"Okay, guys," David said. "Then, I'm off to practice, I guess. But the next time I see you guys, you'd all better be alive and well… and have the dirt on the Firefly Bandits. Okay?"

"We guarantee it," Safia assured.

Once back in her car, Zuri Walker wasted no time taking a sample from the blood in the handkerchief and inserting it into the analyzer extension of her computer. She began the program right away and said to herself, "Okay, Safia Douglas. Let's see if you're the one I'm looking for." Zuri Walker drove away from Tweed-Johnson High School as the computer did its job, and she returned to her office with a sense of accomplishment. The excitement over getting an actual blood sample and the ability to check it against a data base of other samples was almost more than she could stand.

"Hey, Dad!" Safia called. "How's your day been?"

Chief Douglas motioned for his daughter to come on into his office as he said, "A little frustrating, but not too bad."

"And how's your burns feeling?"

"Funny thing… they burn. At times it feels like I'm still being burnt. But at other times, it's not so bad. The doctors were right. It looks a lot worse than it is."

"And your eyes?" Safia probed carefully.

"They're fine. A little scratchy feeling in this right one, but I feel like I'll be fine in no time."

"Well, can you see good enough to read and sign this?"

"And what exactly is this?" Chief Douglas asked his daughter.

"It's a permission form so that this organization can look at my academic records and match me with scholarships, grants, college programs, and stuff like that."

"Oh, wow. That sounds real great. Let me see it. Okay, what do we have here?"

Daniel Douglas took the form and looked it over as Safia scanned the desk. At first she thought she was going to have to try something fancy to get her dad's attention elsewhere. But suddenly she found it… in plain sight.

"Got it!" Sam's voice rang in the hidden earpiece Safia wore. Success was an amazing feeling, and Safia sported a huge smile. Daniel Douglas looked up at his daughter and said, "It means that much to you, does it?"

"Yes, sir. I'm gifted in math."

"I know."

"You do?"

"Yeah, Babydoll. Me and your mom, we've always known there was something extra special about you. I'm glad you discovered it for yourself. But I think I'll wait and let your mom look it over with me tonight when she gets home. She works late tonight, so we probably won't get to it before you go to bed. But don't you worry about that. We'll get it done. But here. Take this back before it gets lost on my desk, and we'll look at it when I get home. Okay?"

"Yes, Sir." Safia turned to walk out, but stopped at the door and added, "Hey, Dad?"

"Yeah, Babydoll?"

"I love you."

"I love you, too, Babydoll."

"Bye!" Safia called over her shoulder as she scampered away to meet Sam and Kenji. The mission, so far, was going as planned. This was quite possibly the best day of Safia's life, and nothing was going to ruin it now.

Back at her office, Zuri Walker looked on as the computer did its work analyzing the data. Suddenly, an alert showed on the screen that made her nearly fall out of her chair, and she quickly sat up and began typing at the keyboard. "You have got to be kidding me," she said in unexpected, stunned disbelief.

"What is it?" Mathew asked, perplexed by her response.

Zuri Walker picked up her phone and placed a call. As soon as the person on the other end answered, she said, "Deputy Director? I just got a hit on a little girl I've been following here in Atlanta, name's Safia Douglas. According to DNA analysis, there is a ninety-nine point nine nine six probability that she is the granddaughter of someone whose DNA we collected from a crime scene back in nineteen seventy-one. Sir... it's Shusk. Safia Douglas is the granddaughter of the Superhuman Serial Killer."

"So, remember," Kenji said, "you are not going in to be a superhero today... you're just going in so we can get pictures of evidence to give to the police... anonymously... so they can get a warrant and make the arrests."

"And I'll see everything you see," Sam reassured. "Plus, I've tapped into the live feeds of every security camera in the immediate vicinity. If anything moves for several blocks, I'll be watching it."

"And I'll be your eyes and ears on the ground," Kenji said. "I'll be right around the corner if you need back-up."

"Then, let's do this," Safia said as she adjusted the mask and started around the corner to the apartment building of the suspected leader of the gang.

Nate Douglas looked on, undetected by the kids, as he held a shiny metal object in his hand. He whispered to himself, "You fool kids gonna make me do somethin' I don't wanna do." Clinching the shiny metal object even tighter, he shed a few tears as he concluded, "But I don't even got a choice, do I? I don't even got a choice. You kids ain't givin' me a choice."

As Safia approached the house, Sam looked on through the mask-cam and then checked the feed from the security cameras in the area. "Okay," Sam assured, "the coast is clear."

"What does that mean anyway, the coast is clear?" Kenji asked.

"Guys!" Safia whispered forcefully. "Cut out the unnecessary chatter and stay on task!"

"You sound like Mrs. Gramble," Sam responded.

"Well... I guess I do. What do you got on surveillance?"

"All the security cameras in the area show no activity, no one walking, nothing. Kenji, what do you have?"

Kenji replied, "I got a perfect view from where I am, and it looks pretty clear to me."

"Okay. Then I'm goin' in," Safia decided. Safia forced the door open with a little of her super strength and slipped into the apartment. The front door gave way to the living room, and she began to survey the tables and corners, all covered with trash and dirty laundry. "This guy's a slob."

"That's for sure," Sam agreed.

"Never mind that," Kenji redirected. "You're not here to critique his housekeeping habits. You're here to find evidence. And you're probably not gonna find it in the living room. Look for a back room, or an unused bedroom, or something like that."

"Okay," Safia acknowledged.

Outside and across the street, Kenji took a quick look around to make sure he wasn't drawing any suspicion. He didn't notice Nate Douglas watching his every move. Nate had a look of deep, internal conflict on his face as he stepped into an alley and went behind a dumpster before crouching down and reaching into his bag. "Those kids are fools," he muttered to himself. "And they're all gonna die."

Safia looked into the closet of the extra bedroom and noticed a set of garments hanging in the middle of an otherwise empty closet. She slid the garments aside to see what looked like a door. "Do you see that, Sam?"

"I sure do. That panel looks like a door." As Safia reached to remove the panel, Sam cautioned, "Saf, be careful."

Safia paused for a moment to reassure her friend, "I will." She reached on further until the panel was in her grasp, and she gently pried it from the wall. Sure enough, there was a hole in the wall that led into the empty apartment next door. Safia climbed through the hole and found the criminals' lair complete with maps, supplies, and loot. "Sam? You gettin' this?"

"Yes, Ma'am. I sure am." Safia looked on with amazement at what she saw. "Remember, you don't need to get anything. Just let me get a clear look at it through the camera.

"Okay. Go ahead," Safia responded.

"Hold on just a second longer while I compensate for the poor lighting."

"Okay but hurry it up. I wanna get out of here before anyone comes back."

"Hey, guys!" Kenji interjected.

"Yeah?" Safia responded.

"There's a car pulling down the alley. And it's slowing down like it might stop in back of the apartment."

"Okay. Sam, you got it?" Safia asked with nervous energy abounding.

"Yeah! I got it! Get out of there!"

Safia quickly stepped back through the hole and replaced the panel. As she slid the garments back in front of the panel, she heard Kenji whisper forcefully, "Saf, they stopped right at the back door and they're getting out! You need to hurry!"

"I'm hurrying as fast as I can!" she whispered back as she skipped through the apartment.

As she scampered through the living room, the back door opened and one of the entrants said, "What was that noise?"

Safia ran out the front door, slamming it behind her in her hurry. She was quickly pursued by two fellows who were angrily yelling at her, "Stop, you stinkin' kid! You can't rob us! Get back here!"

Safia ran down the half flight of steps to the front door of the building and made her way outside. "Which way should I run?" she asked in desperation.

"To the right!" Sam responded. Safia began running to the right as Sam continued, "There's a parking complex on the other end of the block. Run in there and find a place to hide."

"Okay!" She ran quickly to the parking complex, speed being an attribute her tiny frame had always possessed. She went into the complex and ran up the stairs to the third floor. There she paused to catch her breath and calm down a little. "You see me?"

"Yeah. I got you on security cams. You're good. Just wait right there and I'll tell you when they're gone."

"Okay." Safia stood still next to a concrete pillar and tried to control her breathing.

Finally, Sam said, "They're gone, Saf. They're gone."

Kenji confirmed, "Yeah, I just saw them run right past the parking complex and it looks like they're headed into the Chinese restaurant. You did it. You got the evidence and you got away. Good work."

Safia smiled with relief and a sense of accomplishment. She stepped out from behind the concrete pillar and started back toward the stairs. "Saf, wait!" Sam alerted.

"What is it?"

"There's a car moving way too fast headed for your level."

Safia went on the guard as she heard the screeching of tires and saw the car turn the corner from the fourth level, headed her way. She had nowhere to run, no time to run. So she boldly reached out and stopped the car with her hands. She slid backward for some fifteen feet before lifting the car's front tires off the ground.

"Saf, that's it!" Sam exploded with amazement. "It's a front-wheel drive! They can't do anything now!"

The front tires stopped turning and Safia violently and unceremoniously dropped the front of the car to the floor, rattling the occupants and forcing them to flee. As one of them fled, the other suddenly turned and pulled out a gun, pointing it right at Safia.

"Deke, what you doin' man?" cried the other man who had fled. He stopped running long enough to try to reason with his partner in crime. "She's just a kid! And we don't kill people!"

"Not my call!" Deke reasoned aloud. "Johnny said she was inside the apartment! So we can't afford to let her live! If she tells the police what she saw, they'll have us for real this time!"

"Deke, no!" the other man pled.

"I got no choice!" Deke said as he walked ever closer to Safia. "It's her or me! And given that choice, I choose me!" Deke pulled the trigger at almost point-blank range.

A large, ebony hand reached in front of the gun and caught the bullet before it could reach Safia's body. Both Safia and Deke looked on with amazement as a superhero in full uniform stood next to them, bullet in his hand. "Now, you don't really want to do that, do you?" the superhero said.

"A-Power?" Deke said in fearful awe.

"Well now if you know who I am, shouldn't you be runnin'?" A-Power replied with a snarl.

Deke started running backward, of sorts, and almost stumbled over the car before turning to run like a frightened cat. In only moments, there was no sign of either of the men from the car.

"A-Power?" Safia asked in awe.

"You know I hate that name."

Shaking her head as if clearing cobwebs, Safia stuttered, "I—I'm—I'm sorry. Shujaa Nguvu?"

"Yeah. Now that's my name," he said as he rubbed his hand, the hand that caught the bullet. "That didn't used to hurt like that. Mmm, that hurts!"

"I—I don't know what to say," Safia said.

"Well, you could start by explainin' this harum-scarum plan you kids hatched and how you thought this was a good idea. You could have been killed, or worse."

"Worse?" Safia puzzled.

"And do you realize you were committing a crime? Breaking and entering is a felony in Georgia and can get you twenty years depending on the DA you get, and I wouldn't count on your mother gettin' you out of trouble."

"Wait… Pop?" Safia exclaimed with disbelief.

"Yes… Pop." Leaning into Safia's face, Nate smiled and waved as he said, "Hi, Samantha." Sam was amazed and rocked back in her seat at the secret room. "Now," continued Nate Douglas, "let's go get Kenji and we'll all wait for David in your not-so-secret room." Safia's mouth slowly opened with awe as she realized how amateur the circle of friends must be.

A-Power and the masked girl quickly made their way through the shadows and unseen places. Sam said, "Saf, where did you guys go? I can't see you on any cameras."

Commander A-Power said, "And you can tell your friend to stop looking for us because we're not gonna walk where the cameras can see us. That would defeat the purpose, now wouldn't it. Also, you might want to ask her if she's aware that she could go to state or even federal prison for hacking into security cameras… depending on the cameras she hacks."

They avoided detection until they came up behind Kenji, who was looking across the street trying to find them. A-Power put his hand on Kenji's shoulder, making him jump a little. "And what exactly do you call yourself doin'? It can't be standin' guard if an old, washed-up grandpa like me just snuck up on you with his untrained granddaughter in tow."

"Hi, Pop," Kenji said in shame. "Uhm, I'm... the back-up?"

"You're the back-up?" Nate asked with sarcasm.

"Um, yes, Sir."

"And just how are you the back-up, son?"

"Well... I know martial arts?"

"Uh huh, and if you had to engage in combat, just where is your mask?"

"Uh... I didn't think about that."

"Yeah, there's a lot you kids didn't think about. Come on." As they walked away, A-Power pulled out his cell phone and made a call. "Hey. It's time for a meeting. Everybody. I'll bring the kids." Safia and Kenji looked at each other, unsure of what was going on.

Eighteen minutes later, David ran into the secret room, unaware of the events which had unfolded. "Come on, guys. You never texted me back. How did it..." David began as he locked eyes on Commander A-Power sitting with his three friends. "Holy moly!" he exploded with child-like excitement. "Are you for real? Is this... is this real?"

Commander A-Power removed his mask to reveal Nate Douglas and responded, "Son, you have no idea how real this is."

Find out what happens next in

SHUJAA SAFARA
And the Return of the Mashujaa
Books 2 and 3

ACKNOWLEDGMENTS

I would like to thank…

…God first of all for making me a little different from everyone else. I have always had an active imagination, and I've probably spent far too many hours of my life entertaining myself in my own mind with my own stories. When I was a kid, I wrote short stories, always fiction, always trying to be clever. A bad experience in middle school made me hate reading (and to an extent, writing as well), and it wasn't until my mid-thirties that I rediscovered my love of reading, both fiction and non-fiction alike. Finally, in my early- to mid-forties, I realized that I wanted to write fiction again, whether anyone else enjoyed the stories as much as I did or not. Once I started writing, I realized that God made me this way because, among the other things He intended for me to be, He meant for me to be a storyteller, to entertain the people around me with the creations from my unique imagination. Everything I was as a child, am now, and ever will be, whatever is true, whatever is honest, whatever is just, whatever is pure, whatever is lovely, whatever is of good report, whatever is virtuous or worthy of any praise, it is God working in me. To Him be all glory, and honor, and power, and praise, for ever and ever. So let my life reflect His goodness in me, and God help my imperfections that You are yet to, but I am confident faithful to, remedy in me.

…my loving wife, Jessica. Aside from salvation full and free by faith through the blood of Jesus Christ, you are the single greatest gift God has ever given me. You are my perfect match in every possible way, complementing my strengths while simultaneously scaffolding and challenging my weaknesses. Loving you has been my greatest honor aside from Christ, and I know that I am a better man because of the life I have shared with you.

...our children, Lizzie, Katie, and Daniel. You have each enriched our lives while challenging us to grow in ways I thought impossible. I have seen you overcome obstacles, setbacks, and redirections in life, and through it all you have grown up, adapted, and persevered. I anxiously await the future that assuredly lies before each of you, hoping that God will grant your mother and me many years of old age to watch you all soar where even eagles dare not fly. You are each meant for something wonderful, far too grand to be seen by the eyes of the present. Discover your purpose, embrace it, and live it.

...my parents, Payton and Linda. You have always been my biggest fans, no matter what it was that I was doing. Music, theatre, show choir, singing groups, entrepreneurialism, evangelism, pastoring, karate, school bus driving, going back to college in my forties, becoming a math teacher, writing again... you were always there believing that I was the best at whatever I did, even when I wasn't. You always believed in me, as good parents do. My friends at college were always amazed when I told them that I never snuck out of the house growing up. I just explained to them that you don't sneak out of good homes, you stay in bed and sleep peacefully with a thankful heart. Thank you for the home in which I was raised and reared. I wish everyone could have a home like ours was.

...my brothers, Jeff and Patrick. Being the youngest of three boys wasn't always easy, and I made it worse by being generally irritating and nosey. I'm glad you didn't kill me when we were kids (although I think Patrick had a few really good excuses along the way that would have held up in court, a certain broken toy comes to mind). It couldn't have been easy being my older brothers. Thank you for putting up with me, teaching me, protecting me, chauffeuring me around, and letting me grow up to be my own man. You two helped shape the person I have become, for better or worse, and I am grateful to be your brother. I only wish we could spend more time together these days, because I miss hanging with you guys.

...my sister, Rachel. Thank you for bringing your family into our lives and making it so much richer. Thank you for being a living example of perseverance, determination, and courage to change. You inspire me. You are now and forever will be wǒ de fēng kuáng de mei mei.

...all my family, near and far. I love you very much.

...Boykin Church of God. You supported me when I went back to college, you have supported me as I have worked on my writings, we survived Hurricane Michael and covid together, and though we are now small in number, we are big in heart. God bless us all with His best for His glory.

...my many coworkers and students who believed in me. Thank you all.

COMING SOON

Tadashi Mamoru And The Cursed Swords Of The Sacred Temple

The exciting next installment of The Mashujaa series, *Tadashi Mamoru And The Cursed Swords Of The Sacred Temple* takes Kenji Nakajima and his family home to Japan, back to their family's origin, and deep into danger. What family secrets will be discovered when the most sacred duty of the Nakajima family is finally revealed to its youngest member? Why must this secret be kept from the Mashujaa? Where is Kenji's brother, Katsuo? And what is the secret of the cursed swords hidden in the Temple of Tsuyoi Hōmon-sha?

Shujaa Safara And The Crest Of Sirclantis

The third installment of The Mashujaa series, *Shujaa Safara The Crest Of Sirclantis* takes the Douglas family to Chicago, Illinois, U.S.A., to investigate the disappearance of the one who has been selected to be the next Bearer of the Crest of Sirclantis. Our heroes suddenly find themselves in extreme peril as they match wits and strength with a serial killer who hunts superhumans. What's worse? This superhuman has become the most powerful of all superhumans, desperate for more power at the expense of his victims. Will they all survive this encounter? Will anyone help them? And how can they defeat an enemy who is much, much stronger than them and always one step ahead?

Self-Aware: The Dawn Of E.V.E.

The first in the Self-Aware series, *Self-Aware: The Dawn Of E.V.E.* follows the life of amnesiac Adam Tercero, a local TV cameraman who dreams of people from the past but can never remember who they are. In a time when ASBs, intelligent robots, are used to perform everyday tasks to improve human life and income, Adam finds himself torn between loyalty to his friends and fiancée, who want him to be against these machines, and his gut that tells him that these machines are more than they seem and are worthy of fair treatment. As a socially and politically powerful ASB emerges from the shadows, leading the machines to fight for equality, Adam is forced to choose a side. But is he on the right side? Is he truly free to choose sides for himself, or is he trapped? And are these machines just realistic works of art with impressive programming, or are they actually self-aware?

Harmonic Space: Phase To An Alternate World

The first in the Harmonic Space series, *Harmonic Space: Phase To An Alternate World* follows nineteen-year-old college student Lynn Wilson, a brave young woman trying to navigate the difficulties of moving into adulthood without parents to guide her. Just as she begins to settle into life as a collegiate, her father, imprisoned for killing her mother fourteen years earlier, manages to earn parole, and he promptly interjects himself into her life. Constantly trying to get her to believe things that are impossible, Lynn's father tells her that he is on a quest to bring her mother back. Returning to the cabin in the Nunavut Territory in Northern Canada where her mother vanished when she was just a child, Lynn discovers that her father may not be as insane as everyone believes. Perhaps her mother really did travel to a parallel universe through a portal that she and Lynn's father opened together. Did her mother phase shift from this reality to another? Has she been trapped in another universe all these years? If so, is she still alive? And can Lynn and her father bring her home? And who is this dangerous militant group following close behind who wants to claim the portal and the alternate universe for themselves? And what secrets lie in the next harmonic space?

ABOUT THE AUTHOR

Jeremiah Cornet is a simple man who wanted to solve a problem. He loved fiction, especially science fiction, but really didn't like how a lot of fictional works contain a large amount of profanity or are written on a level that is either too unrealistic and childlike or realistic but too inappropriate for younger audiences. Seeking to find a balance, he started writing his first book, *Self-Aware: The Dawn Of E.V.E.*, and quickly fell in love with writing his stories. Now an author with multiple books in tow, Jeremiah Cornet seeks to leave the controversial language and subjects in the social and political arenas where they belong and, instead, simply provide good, wholesome, intelligent, high-quality entertainment to his readers. The inspiration for his stories? Now, that's the stuff of dreams... literally. "I got the idea for the Self-Aware series from a dream. One scene... it stuck with me for days. So I created a story around it. Same goes for the Harmonic Space series. I had a dream... one scene... made a story around it. As for the Mashujaa series, that one was different. I was thinking to myself one day, 'Why do all female superheroes that are strong seem like jerks? Overkill! If I ever wrote a strong female superhero, she'd just be a simple girl, not a jerk. Just a lady with power and conviction.' That's how Safia was born in my mind. Then, I made a story around her."

Printed in the United States
by Baker & Taylor Publisher Services